FAMILY TWIST

By Bonita Y. McCoy

Copyright © 2020 by Bonita Y. McCoy
Published by Gordian Books, an imprint of Winged Publications

Editor: Cynthia Hickey
Book Design by Winged Publications

All rights reserved. No part of this publication may be reproduced, stored in a retrieval system, or transmitted in any form or by any means—electronic, mechanical, photocopying, recording, or otherwise—without the prior written permission of the publisher. The only exception is brief quotations in printed reviews. Piracy is illegal. Thank you for respecting the hard work of this author.

This book is a work of fiction. Names, characters, Places, incidents, and dialogues are either products of the author's imagination or used fictitiously.
Any resemblance to actual persons, living or dead, or events is coincidental. Scripture quotations from The Authorized (King James) Version.

Fiction and Literature: Inspirational
Christian Cozy Mystery

ISBN: 978-1-952661-25-9

Dedicated to:

My three sons
Who taught me all about being a mom and the joy that comes with it
"Behold, children are a heritage from the Lord, the fruit of the womb a reward."
Psalm 127:3

CHAPTER ONE

"What do you mean you found a dead body in a pothole?" I stood between two sets of bookshelves in my bookshop, Twisted Plots, and held the phone away from my ear as a hysterical Julia Jacobs repeated herself.

"Whoa, whoa, back up a minute, Julia. Calm down and start again." I stopped straightening the books on the self-help shelf and gave her my full attention.

Flora, my sixty-something assistant, stopped what she was doing to listen to my end of the conversation. She couldn't resist good gossip. It was her one flaw. Her link to the Pine Lake grapevine, though, had saved me a few times when I found myself entangled with trouble, which happened more often than I care to mention.

"Your Uncle Cyrus found a body in a pothole? Really, Julia, I don't think an entire body could fit in a pothole. Not even the ones here in Alabama."

I looked at Flora who mouthed, 'Uncle Cyrus?'

When I nodded yes, she rolled her eyes.

"No, I'm not trying to give you any grief. I just don't understand how a whole body could fit in a pothole."

Her voice rose two octaves, and I jerked the phone away from my ear. Julia, my best friend and roommate—

calm, respectful, optimistic Julia—was letting me have it.

"Okay, tell me where you are, and I'll come meet you."

Flora held the feather duster in her hand midair and leaned closer to the phone. I scowled at her. She shrugged her shoulders and whisked away a fluff of something from off the dark wood shelf with a flick of her wrist.

"Oh, out by Dead Man's Curve." No one local needed directions to Dead Man's Curve, especially me. I had a plethora of emotions tied to that stretch of road. That's where my mother died in a hit-and-run accident. They never caught the bum.

"I'm on my way."

The instant I pushed the end button, Flora asked, "What happened, Amy Kate? Did you say something about a body?"

"Julia's Uncle Cyrus seems to have found a dead body in a pothole out by Dead Man's Curve. Right before you turn into his driveway. Well, I mean he and Julia, who's with him. She took him to the hospital this morning for his two-weeks checkup for his broken foot. But I don't see how they could have found a body."

"Actually, it *is* possible." Flora followed me to the checkout counter next to the children's section.

"Really?" I doubted it, but I'd hear her out.

"No, it's possible they found something. The city has been doing some construction on the roads out that way. They're digging trenches to lay new pipes to help the drainage problem. They had to bust up some of the roadway and dig pass the existing easements. There used to be a stand of trees at the front of Cyrus's property years ago. Maybe he found something in that area."

"Maybe. I'd better go, though. Julia sounded upset. She's worried about Cyrus." I retrieved my purse from my desk in the back workroom.

Flora leaned against the doorframe and called down

the hall after me. "Yeah, I can imagine since he found a body. He's probably got himself all worked up. Cyrus hasn't been quite right in a long time, though. The Jacobs family worries about him."

"I know. It breaks my heart every time I see him out digging through other people's trash looking for those old glass jars. He's obsessed with those things. Says he puts money in them. Can you imagine that? Money in old pickle jars?" I passed Flora and reentered the main area of my bookshop.

"He is... a bit eccentric," Flora said, which was a nice southern way of saying crazy.

"You'd think at his age he wouldn't be out digging around at all hours of the night. He must be close to eighty. A few weeks ago, I saw him outside of this store around eleven o'clock. Scared me to death. He just appeared in the alley. Said he finds some of his best jars behind the Beans and Leaves Coffee Shop."

"Well, the Jacobs family has tried to do right by him, but he won't let them help him any. He's as stubborn as a mule."

"Speaking of the Jacobs, I'd better go see what I can do for Julia. She'll be wondering what took me so long. Can you hold down the store while I'm gone, or should I call Carter to come in early?"

"You go ahead. I'll be all right here alone. It's been kind of slow today, so I think I can keep the store from burning down." She laughed at her own remark because it'd only been a few months since a fire had damaged my beloved bookshop and forced us to close for a few weeks. But thanks to Mr. Shine and his helper, Ben, it hadn't taken too long for Twisted Plots to be back up and running.

I pointed my old blue van towards the north end of my hometown, Pine Lake, Alabama, toward Dead Man's Curve which sat near the banks of the Tennessee River.

Emotions swelled in me when I drew near the river

where the hit-and-run that took my mother's life six years ago had taken place. My chest tightened, and without thinking, I held my breath until I passed.

Approaching the area on Crestwood Road a few feet from Dead Man's Curve, I spotted Julia standing with her Uncle Cyrus leaning over a rather large, gaping hole. Her car was parked in Cyrus's gravel driveway that led past a stand of trees to his house and forty acres filled with apple trees. He owned a small orchard and had worked the land for as long as I could remember.

A few of the members of the construction crew stood around Julia and Cyrus.

I parked the van close to Julia's car, and she waved me over.

"Hey, I got here as quick as I could."

"Thanks." Julia pointed into the hole. "See for yourself. Uncle Cyrus has found a body."

"Well, actually, Julia, it's a skeleton." Uncle Cyrus said. "Hey gal, how are you today?" Cyrus called all females *gal* and all males *partner*, and everyone in Pine Lake called him Uncle Cyrus.

"I'm all right. How about you, Uncle Cyrus?"

"It'd been a pretty good day until we found this." He pointed to the skeleton. "One of the crew says they called the police. But I wanted you to take a look at it, so I told Julia to call you."

"You should think about a cell phone, Uncle Cyrus," Julia remarked.

"I don't want one of those confounded mobile phones. It's stupid when a man's pants pocket vibrates. In my day, it'd be considered downright vulgar." Julia and I smothered a laugh.

Stubborn rang in my ears from my conversation with Flora. She's right. He was a hundred percent mule.

Peering down into the hole, I could see pieces of skeleton sticking up. "Are we sure it's a human skeleton?"

I asked Julia.

"Look closer," she said.

I kneeled on the pavement, thankful I'd worn jeans on this warm May day and used my phone as a flashlight. The light bounced off the straight bones of the arm that were most prominent, and when I ran the light down the bone, I noticed a hand protruding out of the rubble. With a little maneuvering, I ran the light along the walls of the hole and spotted a human skull. "I see what you mean."

"Yeah." Julia crossed her arms.

"Hey, hand me that stick over there," I said to her. Uncle Cyrus stood back a little, leaning on his crutches and watched.

Julia found a stick in the pile of cleared trees and handed it to me. "What are you doing?"

"There's something on the hand. It's the right hand. It might be a ring of some sort." I pushed the stick down into the hole and jiggled the bones around a bit. They fell to pieces with the movement. The metal thing that had been on the hand rolled a few inches from the skeleton, and I could see for sure it was a ring. "I need a thinner stick." I glanced up at Julia. "It's a ring, but this stick is too thick to fit inside it, and if I mess with it too much, I'll lose sight of it and damage the skeleton more, and you know how Gabe will feel about that."

"Yes, I do." Julia walked in a small circle searching for a thinner yet sturdy stick. She found one close to a mound of red clay dirt piled to the side of the construction. "Here, see if this one will work."

Uncle Cyrus moved to stand behind me, peering over my shoulder, his crutches inches from my knees. "What is it?"

"Think I found a ring," I answered. After several attempts to fish it out, I finally slipped the ring onto the stick. "Look, I got it." I held the ring up to show them.

"Let me see that." Cyrus snatched the ring out of my

hand. "Oh no, no, no," he murmured. "It can't be. It just can't."

I rose from my kneeling position and stared at him. Uncle Cyrus's face turned ash white.

"What is it?" I flung my arms around him to brace him and gave Julia a questioning look. She appeared to be as confused as I was.

Julia moved to him. "What is it, Uncle Cyrus? What's wrong?"

"It's Mildred's ring. I can't believe it."

"How do you know it's Mildred's ring?" Julia asked.

"Because I gave it to her on our tenth anniversary. I had it made special for her. Diamonds and emeralds in a gold band. She loved this ring."

Julia turned pale and gasped. "You mean that's—" She cut her eyes toward the hole.

"Julia, who is Mildred?" I asked.

"She was Uncle Cyrus's wife who left him over thirty years ago. I've only heard rumors. I never met her. She left before I was born." Julia shook her head.

Cyrus's knees gave way, and he leaned his body against me. Tears trickled down the valleys of his wrinkled cheeks. "I thought she was lost to me forever, but I knew she'd never leave. I knew it."

The red Corvette stopped along the side of the road, not too far from the broken stretch of ground. Lieutenant Gabe Cooper of the Pine Lake Police Department jumped out and strolled toward the group. A couple of the men from the road crew remained. The others had moved further up the road to continue working.

Julia, Cyrus, and I watched as the detective approached.

"Amy Kate Anderson, I should've known I'd find you here." A lopsided grin appeared on his lips. "So, I understand you've found a body?"

Even under these circumstances, the man looked handsome. We'd only been dating since January when my bookshop was damaged in a fire, but he made my heart race every time I saw him.

"A skeleton, to be more precise." Julia nodded in the direction of the hole.

Gabe stopped and peered in. "Hm, I see. It's been here for a while by the looks of it."

"Yeah, and I might have disturbed a few things when I fished this out." I showed him the ring.

"You tampered with the body?" Gabe's brows furrowed. "You know better than to touch anything at a crime scene. I expected more from a former police detective's daughter." Gabe pulled out a notebook. "Okay, tell me what happened."

Tears drifted down the creases in Uncle Cyrus's weathered face. He swiped at them with his handkerchief, but it did little good. "Well, we were on our way home from the hospital—me and Julia." Uncle Cyrus cleared his throat and glanced toward the remains. "And we noticed all the workers standing around this hole. I thought they might have busted a pipe, and I wanted to check to see if I'd have water when I got up to the house." His voice shook.

"We pulled over," continued Julia, "and discovered that it was a skeleton."

Uncle Cyrus nodded, fighting the tears. "Then Amy Kate came and found the ring." His eyes filled again, and his hands shook against the crutches. "It's my Mildred. She's been here all this time."

Julia and I exchanged glances. I couldn't imagine the pain he felt after all these years to find her here, like this.

Gabe placed a hand on the older man's shoulder. "How do you know who it is, Cyrus?"

"The ring," Cyrus answered.

Gabe stood straight and held out his palm. "Let me see that."

I handed it to him, grateful, he hadn't mentioned anything about charging me with tampering with evidence. "He says he had it made for his wife, Mildred, for their tenth anniversary. He seems pretty sure this is the same ring." I caught Gabe's eye and nodded toward Cyrus. "Is it okay if they go on up to the house? It might be good if he can get off his broken foot."

Gabe glanced at each one of them and then nodded his consent. "I'll be up in a few minutes to talk to you. I need to call the coroner out here first. I'm sure they'll want to send the skeleton to the state forensic team in Huntsville."

Julia placed her hand on Cyrus's arm. "Can you make it to the car, or do you need help?"

One of the work crew offered to follow them to her car.

Once alone with Gabe, I asked, "Do you think it's her? According to Julia, she's been missing for thirty years."

Gabe jotted something down in his notebook and closed the flap, returning it to the inside pocket of his suitcoat. Then he pulled out a plastic bag, deposited the ring in it, and poked it back into his inside pocket. "I don't want to start guessing. Let's wait for the forensic report. I'm sure if it is Mildred Jacobs, they'll be able to identify her by her dental records."

"That sounds reasonable." I peered down into the hole.

Gabe walked over and stood beside me, tucking a stray blonde hair behind my ear. "Amy Kate, I don't want you to get any ideas about this. I know you love a good mystery but leave this alone." His soft brown eyes looked like melted chocolate, warm and sweet. I wanted to swear to him I'd stay out of it, but since Julia's family was involved, I'd be right in the thick of things. After all these years, didn't Uncle Cyrus deserve to know how his wife came to be buried on the edge of their property? And didn't he need to know who was responsible for putting her there?

So, I pressed my lips together and smiled. Besides,

how much trouble could I get into? It'd been over thirty years. Clearly ancient history, right?

CHAPTER TWO

We found Cyrus and Julia in the library of Uncle Cyrus's two-story home. Cyrus had his foot propped up on a footstool that matched the material of the Queen Anne chair he sat in. Julia leaned against the large oak desk holding a mug.

Gabe took the leather chair adjacent to Cyrus near the fireplace, and I pulled a smaller leather chair over from in front of the desk. A statue of an elephant the size of a trophy sat on the corner of the desk and caught my eye. It was white and looked out of place compared to the other knickknacks in the room.

Cyrus sipped on a cup of hot tea.

"Are you feeling better, Cyrus? Up for a talk?" Gabe leaned his forearms on his knees and clasped his hands together. "I need you to tell me what you remember about your wife's disappearance. I know it's been a while, though, and you might be a little fuzzy on the details."

"Fuzzy on the details?" Cyrus snapped, his eyes hard. "I'll never forget that weekend. It's seared into my brain."

"All right." Gabe leaned back into the chair and crossed his ankle over his knee. He pulled out his notebook and pen. "When you're ready."

Cyrus closed his eyes and leaned his head back against the chair. "It was a Friday afternoon. Mildred had packed that morning to go on a women's retreat with two friends from church. She'd been excited about going earlier in the week, but then something happened, and she wasn't sure she should go. I'd assumed she'd had an argument with one of the ladies. A squabble or something." Cyrus opened his eyes. "You know, over who would stay in which room or something like that."

"Okay." Gabe nodded and jotted down a few notes. "Who were these two friends?"

"Let's see. One's name was Kelly Parnell. She moved to Florida some years ago. But the other one, Beth Mitchell, still lives in town. I think she remarried. Don't know what her last name is now. I didn't keep in touch with them much after—" Cyrus shrugged. "Anyway, I'd gone into Guntersville to see about some new apple trees the nursery had gotten in that week. I was gone all day. It was dark by the time I returned."

"When was the retreat? What month?" I asked.

Gabe shot me a warning look.

"April," Cyrus glanced my way, then turned his attention back to Gabe. "She and her suitcase were gone when I got back. I figured the women had worked out their issues. But when the time for her to return rolled around, she never showed."

Julia stood and moved behind Cyrus's chair. "What did you do when she didn't come home?"

"I phoned Beth. She said Mildred told them she wasn't going, but if she changed her mind, she'd call Friday morning, but Beth said she never called. They'd gone without her." Cyrus hung his head. "I called the police, then I hunted through the closets to see if her suitcase was gone."

"Was it?" Gabe asked.

"Yeah, the suitcase, some of her clothes, and the ring

Amy Kate found today. All gone." Cyrus sighed. "Once the fact that her clothes and a suitcase were missing got out, the rumors of her running off with someone started to circulate, but I didn't believe them. Mildred and I had been happily married for over ten years. Why would she run off?"

Julia leaned over the back of the chair and placed her hand on Cyrus's shoulder. "That must've been hard for you. Small town gossip can be brutal."

"The worst part was when someone told the police they'd seen Mildred out at the old Martin place talking with Gary Martin."

Gabe's brows furrowed. "Who is Gary Martin?"

"Mildred's high school sweetheart. Shortly before Mildred disappeared, he left town. With him leaving and Mildred's disappearance, there was no stopping the tongues from wagging."

Julia patted Cyrus's shoulders. "I'm so sorry you had to go through all that."

"Do you know what happened to Gary Martin?" Gabe had his pen poised on the paper.

Cyrus straightened in his chair, moving away from Julia's touch. She folded her arms along the back of the chair. "Yeah, he's back here in Pine Lake."

"When did he move back?" I pushed a strand of hair behind my ear.

"Maybe six years ago." Cyrus's lips pulled tight.

It was obvious he didn't want to talk about Gary Martin. Who could blame him? But we needed information if we were going to find out who had buried Mildred on Cyrus's property. "Have you talked with him about this since he moved back?"

Cyrus stiffened and pinched his lips together.

"Look, Uncle Cyrus, I know this is hard. But we need to know," Julia's soft voice pleaded.

"I went to his place a few months after he moved back. His wife met me at the door. When he stepped out onto the porch, I punched him."

Julia rolled her eyes and let out a groan. Lieutenant Gabe Cooper smothered a grin.

Uncle Cyrus was a man of action more than words.

"Then what happened?" Gabe asked.

"He told me he'd heard the rumors and several people had asked him about Mildred, but he swore she was never with him."

Gabe tapped the pen against the notebook. "Did you believe him?"

"Yeah, because I never believed Mildred had run off, but because of this story going around, the police didn't pursue it. They chalked it up to a May-December romance that had run its course." Cyrus leaned back against the chair again, the color drained from his face. "I need to rest a while. If that'd be okay."

Gabe nodded and stood. "Sure. No problem. But I might be back with more questions. The forensic team is going to do a full workup on the bones to see if we can determine the cause of death. Once we have that, I'll need to speak with you again."

Cyrus nodded and closed his eyes, reaching up he touched Julia's hand. "Gal, will you stay with me while I rest?"

"Sure, Uncle Cyrus." Julia kissed the top of the old man's head.

"And you too, Amy Kate. I might need your help to climb the stairs to the bedroom to get my things since I'll be sleeping down here tonight."

"I can gather those for you," Julia said.

"Not my personal things you can't," Cyrus grumbled. "Besides, I want to hear how the plans for the family reunion are going. I need to know who I might be running into if I go. So, I can be ready. I can only imagine the onslaught of questions there'll be now that I've found Mildred."

While Julia helped Cyrus gather his things upstairs, I came back down to touch base with Flora at the bookshop. I sent her a text to make sure Carter had made it in for his evening shift and to let her know about the skeleton.

Flora: I will expect all the juicy details Monday.

Me: Fine. In exchange for anything you might know about Mildred Jacobs.

Flora: Is that who they think it is? Bring cinnamon raisin bread. I'll pick up the coffee.

I hit the thumbs up emoji and sent it, placing my phone back into my pocket.

While I waited for Julia to call me to help with Cyrus, I perused his library. I had to admit, Uncle Cyrus had a great book collection. There were several first editions and a whole shelf of books from the early nineteen hundreds. One or two of the first editions I'd procured for him over the last few months.

An early edition of *Tom Sawyer* caught my eye, and I couldn't resist pulling it from the shelf. The cover was faded, and the edges torn and flaky. At one time, this had been a beloved copy, well used. Opening the flap, I found the frontispiece, an illustration of a boy with a hat, wearing checkered pants sitting under a large tree with his fishing pole in the water. Intrigued, I moved to the Queen Anne chair and took a seat. I gingerly turned the pages, looking at the font used for the chapter headers and the drop letter in the first paragraphs. Old books always gave me the sense of being in the presence of art.

As I turned to the middle of the book to check out the other illustrations, a thin yellowed envelope dropped from the pages. It was addressed to Mildred Jacobs, and it was postmarked 1984. Two years before her disappearance.

I went to open it but heard Julia at the top of the stairs arguing with Uncle Cyrus. "Don't you dare try to come down alone. Am I going to have to take you home with me tonight to make sure you behave?"

"Gal, I've stayed out here on my own for the last thirty years. I'm not letting a little old broken foot make me into an invalid. I won't be going to your tiny apartment—so small I can't turn around in it."

Out of instinct, I flipped through the book to see if there were any more letters. When I didn't find any, I stuffed the envelope into my back pocket and hurried to the bookcase to the right of the fireplace and slid the novel back on the shelf. I met Julia in the hallway.

"Uncle Cyrus is being difficult." Her lips stretched into a straight line, and her bright green eyes flashed disapproval. "We can't leave him here alone. He's going to reinjure his foot, and then it'll be surgery for sure."

"I can hear you, gal. I'm not deaf. Just clumsy."

Julia rolled her eyes. "I'll stay the night and make sure he stays downstairs on the couch. The doctor told him to avoid the stairs if possible. Would you mind putting together an overnight bag for me and bringing it out here?"

"Not at all," I said.

Julia leaned closer and whispered, "He shouldn't be alone after what happened today."

"No, you're right. He doesn't need to be alone. I can't imagine what must be going through his mind."

Uncle Cyrus called down to us, "Am I going to have to stand up here all night, or are you two coming?"

Julia sighed, and we trotted up the stairs double time to keep Uncle Cyrus from attempting them on his own.

Once we settled Uncle Cyrus on the couch in the living room with the TV on a sitcom, Julia followed me out to my van. "I appreciate you doing this for me, Amy Kate."

"No problem. You'd do it for me."

Julia turned to go inside, but the letter in my pocket pricked at my conscience.

"Wait. There's something I need to show you." I pulled the letter out and handed it to her. She examined it in the fading twilight.

"Where did you get this?"

"In the library. I found it stuffed between the pages of *Tom Sawyer*. I haven't read it yet. Considering what happened today, do you think I should?"

Julia ran her finger along her jawline. "I'm not sure. Uncle Cyrus is so private. He'll be boiling mad if he finds out we've been snooping."

"True, but we found his wife's body. You know who the number one suspect will be."

Julia's eyes widened. "Uncle Cyrus."

"Correct. I just want to have a few other suspects to suggest to the police when they start pointing at him."

"Yeah, guess you're right." Julia handed the letter back to me. "Go ahead and read it, and I'll see if I can find anything else that might give us an idea of who would've done this to Aunt Mildred. But I'm not holding out much hope. It's been thirty years."

"I know but try. And call Elizabeth. Let her know what's going on. I have a feeling Uncle Cyrus is going to need a good lawyer, sooner rather than later."

CHAPTER THREE

Julia spent most of the weekend either at Uncle Cyrus's or at work at the Whispering Pines Bed and Breakfast. As the head chef, she put in long hours by day, and then by night, she ran her own bakery, Pure Sweetness. On top of that, she'd been working overtime trying to get everything finalized for the upcoming Jacobs' family reunion.

She'd let herself be talked into doing the food and most of the airport pickups. Luckily, she'd recruited her sous-chef, Miles, and the kitchen staff at the Whispering Pines to help with food prep, and me to help with airport pickup. I, in turn, recruited Carter Cooper, my other over-sixty employee, to chauffeur.

The sticky note on the refrigerator reminded me that several of her family members were scheduled to arrive today. They wanted to help prepare things for Thursday, the official start of the reunion. From Julia's response, she didn't relish their offer of help. Not that she didn't appreciate it, but she knew from experience too many cooks in the kitchen can cause problems.

"Do you have someone picking up my cousins Melissa and Betsy?" Julia asked. "And where is my tablet? I have everything on it." She hunted around the kitchen counters under mail and piles of paper products.

"Yes, Carter agreed to do it for me. He's perfect for the job. I gave him a copy of the schedule you printed for me." I leaned over and picked up Gizmo, my black Scottish terrier, and set him in my lap.

"Don't forget Betsy is bring her fiancé, Jim. So, there will be three of them to fit into the car along with their luggage."

"No problem, remember? I own a van that seats seven comfortably." I grinned at her. "With luggage. Carter can use it for the airport run."

She exhaled and plopped into the chair at our kitchen table. "I'm not going to make it. Between this reunion, the food prep, and the dead body—Oh, and let's not forget the stubborn man in a cast who refuses to take it easy—I'm drowning. And now, I can't find my tablet."

I put down Gizmo, rinsed my hands, and poured the last dregs of the coffee into a mug, then added cream and sugar. "Here, you go. What you need is more caffeine."

"Thanks." Julia wrapped her hands around the mug. "What I need is a good dose of me time with a binge session of my favorite crime show, but that's not going to happen." She leaned back in her chair. "Speaking of crime, I've been meaning to ask you. Did you read that letter?"

"Yes, I did. The envelope was so fragile I had to be careful not to tear it. And the notebook paper inside had yellowed. It was like doing surgery to read it." I grabbed my own mug of coffee from the kitchen counter and joined her at the table. A few minutes remained before I had to leave to pick up the cinnamon raisin bread for Flora. I'd never live it down if I forgot it.

"So, what did it say? Anything interesting?"

"In a way. It was from someone named Carol?"

"Dad has a cousin named Carol. She's around his age. I think her last name is White. She's Great-aunt Emma's daughter, I believe." Confusion washed over her face. "But I could be wrong. Everybody is starting to melt into one blob. Between the hotel reservations and people staying at the inn and all those invitations last month, it's a wonder I can remember my own name."

"Well, it's not important. The letter thanked Mildred for her hospitality. Apparently, Carol had visited. She was telling Mildred what a good time she'd had going strawberry picking with her. It did mention her upcoming wedding to a guy named Percy White. So, you have the last name right." I took a sip of my cold coffee. "Carol had wanted to know if Mildred would come to the wedding. She said several of her family weren't coming because they didn't approve of the marriage, and it would mean the world to her if Mildred would come."

"I wonder if she went." Julia hopped up. "Think I know where my tablet is." She darted out of the kitchen and reappeared a few minutes later with it in hand. "I found it under my pillow. I must've fallen asleep while I was working on the menu for Friday's picnic."

"It's a good thing you took this week off from work. You couldn't do this and work the Memorial Day weekend crowd at the Pines."

Gizmo wandered over to his dog bed, turned three times in a tight circle, then curled up with his head on his paws.

"No," Julia shook her head. "I have all I can do with my own crowd." She grinned and sat back down.

I toyed with the idea of urging Julia to ask Uncle Cyrus about the letter. It would be good to know if Carol and Mildred were close at the time of her disappearance. Maybe Mildred had confided in her about what was bothering her the days leading up to the women's retreat. At least, it might be a place to start. "Is your cousin, Carol, coming to the reunion?"

"Let me check. She tapped the screen on her tablet a

couple of times, swiped her finger across it, and then raised her eyebrows. "Yes, she is."

"You seem surprised."

"I am. It's the first time she's attended a reunion since I was a child. I wouldn't even recognize her if I saw her on the street it's been so long."

"When does she arrive?"

"Wednesday, it looks like they're driving in from St. Louis in their RV. Says here her husband Percy and her son and her older stepson will be joining her."

"Good, then I can ask her about the letter and see what she has to say. I don't relish asking Uncle Cyrus." I went to the microwave to reheat my coffee. "Did you find anything else while you were there Friday night?"

"Not really." Julia wrinkled her nose. "I slept in what I thought was the spare bedroom, but from the jewelry box on the chest of drawers and the pictures sitting out, it might have been the master bedroom, and Uncle Cyrus moved into the guest room after her disappearance. Kind of broke my heart. He's been pining for her all these years."

"Could you imagine not knowing if the person you cared for the most in the world was dead or alive? I don't think I'd stop waiting either," I said.

"Guess you're right. Anyway, I looked through the jewelry box and found a snapshot tucked under one of the trays. It was of a guy in his late twenties at the time of the picture. He wore a baseball hat and was laughing, and he had a mole on his cheek."

"Wonder who it was?"

"No need. His name was written on the back. It was her old sweetheart, Gary Martin."

"He sure does keep turning up, doesn't he?"

"Uncle Cyrus seemed convinced he hadn't been with Aunt Mildred. That all the talk was just that, talk."

"Yeah, but maybe he can tell us who she was close to during the time before she disappeared. They may not have been romantically involved, but something happened that got the town folks to talking. Maybe, he'd be willing to share it now since it's old news."

No sooner had those words dropped from my lips than I opened the *Pine Lake Daily* and discovered the morning headline: Missing Woman Found Dead after Thirty Years.

I jerked the paper down from in front of me and met Julia's gaze. "Did you call Elizabeth?" My sister was the best lawyer in northern Alabama, and from this headline, Cyrus needed the best.

"Yes. Friday night when you suggested it. I knew you were right. Why?"

I placed the paper on the table in front of her.

"Oh."

While she read the article, my phone on the table dinged. A text notification from my sister, Elizabeth, popped up on the screen. I pulled up my text messages and found not one but four. The last one read: *You and Julia meet me at the police station.*

"What is it?" Julia asked.

"We need to go to the police station. Elizabeth needs some help with Uncle Cyrus. I'll call and let Flora know I'll be late coming in, and then we need to go make sure Uncle Cyrus isn't sitting in a jail cell."

Julia leaned back in her chair. "Well at least if he's locked up, he'll be forced to rest." Julia smiled, but it didn't reach her eyes. No, instead, a flicker of worry passed through them. And if I had to admit it, I was a little worried over the situation, too.

The Pine Lake Police Department hummed with activity. Uniformed officers mulled around behind the front desk. One was eating a breakfast burrito and thumbing through a file. I recognized the sergeant on duty talking with an older woman who wore a deep embedded frown.

"I don't care what you say. I know it was the hoodlum

next door who pulled up my petunias."

Sergeant Wallace shook his head. "Ma'am, we talked with the boy, and he didn't know anything about your flowers. Now, this is the third time this week you've been here, and we told you it might be an armadillo doing the damage to your flower beds. Have you called a wildlife removal service?"

The woman lifted her chin and looked down her nose. "It's not an armadillo. It's that boy. But you go ahead and ignore me. Now, it's petunias. Next, it'll be bank robbery. These things always escalate." The woman turned and marched for the door.

Julia and I stepped up to the desk before the sergeant could escape. "Hey, Wallace."

"Hey, Amy Kate. What can I do for you?"

"Is Gabe here?"

"The lieutenant is in but let me call upstairs and make sure."

Julia nudged me with her foot.

"Oh, and do you know if Cyrus Jacobs is here? They haven't brought him in for questioning, have they?"

Wallace chuckled. "I should've known this wasn't a social call. Give me a sec."

Wallace picked up the receiver and pushed a few buttons on the display. He smiled and turned his back to us. I pretended I wasn't listening.

"You have a visitor, Lieutenant." Wallace glanced my way and grinned. "Yup, that's right." He laughed and hung up the receiver. "You can go on up. He said he's been expecting you and was wondering what took you so long." Amusement played in his eyes. "The elevators are—"

"I know ... around the corner." I led the way, and Julia followed.

"Do you think they have Uncle Cyrus? I hope he's all right."

I patted Julia's shoulder. "He'll be fine. Don't worry,

he's a tough old bird."

While I stood outside of the glass doors that led into the squad room, a feeling of dread washed over me. The last time I'd been here I was trying to prove another friend's innocence. How I wished this *was* a social call. I pulled the door open and stepped inside, holding it for Julia. The room smelled of aftershave, old socks, and wait—what was that? Chanel. My sister's perfume.

I scanned the area for Elizabeth and found her standing on the other side of the glass inside one of the interrogation rooms. She had her arms crossed, shaking her head. Cyrus sat across from her, scowling.

Julia nodded in their direction. "I'm going to see if Elizabeth needs my help."

"Good idea. From the looks of it, it's not going well."

"No," Julia said. "It doesn't look good."

"I'm going to see what Gabe's found out. Maybe he's received the forensic report. He'd said he'd need to question Cyrus again when it came in."

Julia headed toward the interrogation room on the right.

Gabe Cooper sat at his desk tapping on his keyboard.

I skirted the other desks that littered the space, an eclectic group, and took a seat in front of him. He peeked around his monitor. "I was wondering when I'd see you today."

"Gloating doesn't become you." I placed my purse on the floor beside the chair leg.

He laughed and pushed his chair away from the desk so he could see me better. "I knew the moment I found you standing over that hole that you couldn't resist getting in the middle of this case."

"Oh, so it's a case now." I crossed my legs. "I see Elizabeth and Cyrus are here."

"Yep, we brought Cyrus in. We had a few questions, but he put up such a ruckus at his house he forced us to haul him down here. But it didn't do any good. He wouldn't talk to us without Elizabeth. We thought she might get some answers out of him."

"Ruckus, huh?"

"The man was going to hit me with one of his crutches. He was so worked up."

"You mean that you, a strong, smart detective, couldn't handle a sweet little old man?" I leaned forward and placed my elbow on the edge of his desk.

His deep brown eyes glistened, and he leaned forward, meeting me halfway. "Now, who's gloating?"

When his dimples appeared one at a time, my heart flip-flopped like a world class gymnast. Then he leaned back in his chair. "I'm glad you brought Julia though. He's been asking for her, and it'll help."

I straightened and let the moment pass. "You aren't arresting Cyrus, are you?"

"No, we don't have anything to hold him on. It's too early in the investigation. We found the suitcase though. It was buried under the skeleton in the same hole."

"What was in it?"

"Clothes, hairbrush, toothbrush, makeup bag, shoes. Exactly what you'd expect to find in a woman's suitcase who was leaving for the weekend. Nothing out of the ordinary." Gabe rubbed his chin. "I do have to say those Samsonite hard-shell cases are tough. The clothes were still intact."

"That's good though, right? That they found the suitcase. You can pull DNA from it to see who threw it in the hole."

Gabe shook his head. "No dice. The killer wiped the handle clean. Not one fingerprint on it. And the few prints the forensic team retrieved from the outside of the suitcase were Mildred's."

"What did the forensic team discover from the bones?" It seemed coldhearted to refer to someone like Mildred as bones.

Gabe's lip lifted in a half grin, and he shrugged.

"So, are you going to share?" I asked.

Gabe pursed his lips and shook his head.

"Can you be bribed?" I asked.

"You know I can." Mischief played in his eyes. "The usual payoff."

"One dozen oatmeal raisin cookies." I figured it was a small price to pay for the information. Besides, I had his mother's recipe, so I had the upper hand any time I needed it.

"The examination of the bones showed it was indeed Mildred Jacobs. They found cause of death to be blunt force trauma," Gabe said.

"English, please."

"Someone hit her in the head, or she fell and hit her head. Either way, it killed her," Gabe said. "And you don't bury a body if it's an accident. The bad part is—" he rested his forearms on his desk and clasped his hands together. "—in cases like this, it's usually the spouse."

I glanced over at the interrogation room. I couldn't picture Cyrus hurting anyone, especially the woman he loved. No, from what Julia said about her things still being out in their bedroom, he didn't kill her. "Cyrus didn't do it. If it's murder, he's not your guy."

"I want to believe that, but I'm going to follow the evidence. And if it leads to Cyrus, I'm going to arrest him." The determination on Gabe Cooper's face showed me where he stood.

I'd have to prove Cyrus's innocence, and my only leads at this point were a long-lost cousin, and unearthed suitcase, and a quick peek at a forensic report, for which I owed the handsome lieutenant a dozen cookies.

Not much to go on. I needed information. It was a good thing I knew where to get it.

CHAPTER FOUR

Carter glanced up from helping a customer when I entered Twisted Plots carrying a loaf of cinnamon raisin bread. He nodded in my direction, and I waved as I passed him, heading toward the back workroom to find Flora.

Flora Smith-Jones was a sixty-something mother of two, grandmother of two, who had come part and parcel with the bookshop, which was sometimes a blessing and sometimes a curse. She knew all about inventory, ordering stock, and Pine Lake, Alabama, which today, I counted as a good thing.

I found her entering inventory into one of the sleek computers housed on the long worktable in the back.

She lifted her head and inhaled. "Something smells wonderful."

"One cinnamon raisin bread loaf as promised. Did you get the coffee?"

She grinned. "Sure did." She looked at her watch. "It's almost eleven. Where have you been?"

"Helping Uncle Cyrus."

"Is he giving you and Julia fits over his broken foot? Men can be such babies when they're hurt. When my Herman has a cold, it's like the world's come to an end."

"No, he's at the police station or was. Elizabeth asked Julia to take him home."

"Police station?" Flora swiveled her stool to face me. "This I've got to hear."

I set the loaf on the workstation and walked over to the kitchen area along the back wall where I fished out two plates and forks from the overflowing pile on top of the mini fridge along with a knife to cut the bread.

Flora retrieved the coffees from my desk and reheated them in the microwave.

In the corner of the workroom sat two overstuffed chairs. I motioned with a paper plate for Flora to take a seat in the second chair. "I'll cut us a piece of bread."

Flora set the coffees on the smallest of the four tables that held my cascade of to-be-read books and plopped into the chair.

I handed her the plate with a slice on it and reached behind my chair to turn on the floor lamp, giving the area a warm glow. Cozy. Perfect for a good heart-to-heart.

By the time I got settled, Flora had eaten half her slice. The woman loved her cinnamon raisin bread.

After a few bites, I asked, "So what can you tell me about Mildred Jacobs?"

"No, you first. What's happening with Cyrus?"

"Gabe went to talk to him about the remains, which has been identified as Mildred Jacobs, and he went berserk. So, Gabe took him to the station and called Elizabeth at his request."

"So, Elizabeth's representing him? That's good." The faraway look in Flora's eyes led me to believe she knew something about it.

"Spill."

Flora heaved a sigh. "Most of what I know is hearsay. Stuff floating around at the time."

"Did you know Mildred?" I took a sip. The coffee tasted delicious. She'd ordered my favorite French Vanilla

Mud from the Beans and Leaves. One of their original flavors.

"Yes, I knew her but not well. We went to the same church at the time, but she attended the older members Sunday School class with Cyrus. So, I didn't get to know her very well even though she was closer to my age."

I nodded but didn't interrupt.

"But she did participate in the women's group. She helped with the annual Christmas bizarre, and she worked the fall carnival. From what I knew of her, she was nice." Flora shrugged.

"So, what did everyone say after she disappeared?"

Flora took a bite before answering. "Well, you can imagine. Some people said she ran off with someone closer to her own age. Apparently, a lot of people didn't care for the fact that Cyrus was fifteen years her senior. Then, there were those who mentioned seeing her with Gary Martin, her high school sweetheart. They were seen together several times over the weeks leading up to her disappearance. That didn't take long to run like fire on the gossip vine."

"Yeah, his name has come up a couple of times already."

"Hm, understandable. They dated all through high school. Everyone expected them to end up together. Others said something happened to her on the retreat. They speculated that Kelly or—" Flora's eyebrows pulled into a sharp V. "What was her name?"

"Beth?" I asked.

"Yes, Beth. Beth Mitchell, but I think she's divorced and remarried."

"You don't happen to remember her new name, do you?"

"Jackson, I believe." Flora placed her empty plate on top of the stack of books and took a sip of her coffee. "Then there were those who believed something terrible had happened to her, like a break-in gone wrong." The lines of Flora's lips pulled taut. "A handful thought Cyrus had murdered her. Can you believe that? Sweet Cyrus murdering someone? They even had the gall to confront him one night at his own house."

I waited for Flora to continue. When she didn't, I asked, "So, you don't think Cyrus is capable of killing anyone?"

"Anyone? I don't know about that, but Mildred, no. He couldn't have ever hurt her." Her tone firm, unyielding.

"Even now that the body has been found on his property?"

Flora shook her head and pressed her lips together so tightly the area around her mouth turned white. She looked as if she were trying to keep a secret from slipping out.

"Do you know something I should know?"

She cut her eyes away from me.

"Flora, what is it?" I scooted forward in my chair and leaned my forearms on my knees. "Tell me."

She hung her head. "That day in April when Mildred was supposed to have disappeared, I drove by Cyrus's property on my way out of town for the retreat." She placed her hand over her heart. "The trees and shrub were thick in front of Cyrus's property, so I don't know how sure I am." She looked up at me, "but I could've sworn I saw Cyrus Jacobs out front with a shovel."

"What do you mean? Why'd you think it was Cyrus?"

"Because whoever it was wore Cyrus's bright orange Tennessee Volunteer jacket."

"Did you tell the police what you saw?"

Flora clasped the paper coffee cup in both hands. "No. I passed by going close to fifty-five miles an hour, and I only caught a glimpse of the person through the trees. I didn't tell them then, and I'm not going to tell them now. And neither are you."

CHAPTER FIVE

On Friday afternoon, Julia rushed around the large, rented tent putting the finishing touches on the picnic luncheon for the Jacobs' family reunion. Whoever decided to have the picnic out at the Pine Lake campgrounds didn't consider the logistical nightmare it would be.

Not only had they needed a tent to house the event due to the forecast of rain but transporting the food out to the tent in the open picnic area near the lake had taken some expert maneuvering on Julia's part, since the parking lot was a mile away.

Staff members of the Whispering Pines Bed and Breakfast buzzed around, setting up the catering dishes and serving utensils, using the Sterno cans to heat the serving dishes since there was no available electricity.

Julia's mother, Cindy, wrestled with the chairs, making sure each table could seat eight comfortably. From my viewpoint, it looked like the chairs were winning. They were from the campground's recreation room and the chairs seemed to be a hodgepodge of metal, plastic, and cloth.

Her Aunt Gloria and her cousin, Melissa, moved from table to table placing the centerpieces created by the florist at The Cracked Flowerpot in their appointed spots. Thomas Jacobs, Julia's dad, stood guard at the tent door, keeping the assembling crowd at bay while Julia gave the area one last look before letting them in to eat.

I stood next to him, acting as a second obstacle.

Julia turned toward me, smiled with her eyes wide, and gave two thumbs-up. I nudged Mr. Jacobs, and we pulled the tent flaps back and secured them with the white ties.

The stream of people swept me up as they entered and deposited me somewhere near the salad bar.

Over the next thirty minutes, the lines moved through the tent at a nice rhythm. One by one the tables filled. I lost track of Uncle Cyrus and searched for him but didn't find him. I spotted Julia talking with her cousins Melissa and Betsy, so I joined them.

"Amy Kate, I was just telling Julia that she needs to plan on doing the cake for my wedding in August," Betsy said.

"Oh, are you getting married here in Pine Lake? I thought you were in Atlanta."

"Both Jim and I adore the little bed and breakfast where we're staying, so why not have the wedding here? It's not like we're tied to having it in Atlanta. Besides, after Julia told me what she spent on this tent, I could do my whole wedding for a fraction of the price if I had it here."

Julia shot me a look which was one-part plea for help and two parts skepticism. "Well, give me the date before you leave, and I'll add it to my calendar," she promised, always the diplomat.

"Have any of you seen Uncle Cyrus? I thought he might need some help getting his food since he's on crutches," I asked.

Melissa pursed her lips and scanned the tables. "I thought I saw him sitting by Great-aunt Emma. He didn't look happy, and neither did she. Of course, Aunt Emma never looks happy."

"You'd think an eighty-year-old man on crutches wouldn't be that hard to find." Following the direction of her gaze, I saw Aunt Emma, Cyrus's older sister, sitting alone at the back table, eating her dessert. But no Uncle Cyrus. "I'll go see how she's doing and see if I can't spot him from there." I moved across the tent toward Aunt Emma, curious why she sat alone in a crowd of her own family.

I pulled the metal chair out and sat down, propping my elbows on the red tablecloth. "How are you, Aunt Emma?"

She scowled at me. "I'm not your aunt, Amy Kate. Maude would be your aunt. And I'm not doing well at all. Why are all these people here?"

Thinking she was confused, I went to answer, but she continued without taking a breath. "I'll tell you why. They want something. They're always standing with their hands out, wanting me and Cyrus to fill them. Thank goodness, our brother, Horace, isn't around any longer to see the despicable state our family has fallen into." The heat of anger tinged her cheeks.

"Why do you say that? The Jacobs family is a hardworking bunch. At least the ones I know."

"Well, be glad you don't know many." She looked out over the crowd, the wrinkles by her eyes accentuating their hardness.

I leaned back in the chair, and the metal squeaked as I shifted my weight. "Speaking of Uncle Cyrus, have you seen him today? I wanted to check on him. See if he's doing all right."

"He was here a few minutes ago, waving those letters around." Her voice rose, and she leaned across the table, pointing her finger at me. "Accusing me of wanting a handout." Her lips tightened into a petite bow. "Can you imagine me needing a handout? How humiliating."

"Letters?" The word struck me. "He had letters?"

"Yes. Didn't you hear what I said?" She tsked. "He demanded to know how long my daughter had been corresponding with his wife. All this nonsense with finding the body has him agitated."

I bit back the remark I wanted to make out of respect for my elders. "Did you tell him?"

"Of course not. I didn't even know they'd been corresponding. Carol never tells me anything about her life beyond the essentials to keep her in my good graces and in my will. Besides, it was years ago."

"So, she tells you what you want to hear." I pressed my lips together, knowing I'd said the wrong thing.

One side of Great-aunt Emma's lips tilted into a half smile. "You have gumption. I like that. But don't abuse it." She straightened. "Carol and I didn't see eye to eye about her choice of husbands when she married Percy. He had a son, and all he wanted was a nanny for the boy and a pocketbook for his habit."

"What habit?"

"I've said too much." She looked me over as if she could find my value written somewhere on a mislaid price tag. "I think Cyrus went to find Carol. You might want to go hunt for him outside. They drove down in their recreational vehicle." She shivered as the last two words rolled off her tongue.

I stood, aware I'd been dismissed, but now at least, I knew there were more letters and possibly a clue as to who had murdered Mildred Jacobs.

The camp site 38C sat further to the back of the campgrounds. The hookups for the RVs included cable in this section, and several people sat outside watching baseball on their outdoor TVs that were built into the sides of their RVs, adding a whole new meaning to the idea of spending time in the great outdoors.

Some of the people waved as I passed, and one little girl on a bike swerved to miss me, then honked the horn attached to her bike handle and scowled.

The tan RV parked in 38C looked like an older model. The stickers and logos curled at the edges, and the paint job had faded due to the years of exposure to the weather. The tattered awning shaded the area in spots, and four camping chairs made a circle around the fire pit to the left side of a dilapidated picnic table. Apparently, her stepson had joined them for the family reunion.

The closer I got to the RV, the clearer the voices from inside became. I recognized one immediately. Uncle Cyrus.

"You can't deny that you wrote these letters, gal. It's your name signed to each one," Uncle Cyrus said.

I stopped outside the open window and listened. My conscience nudged me, but I ignored it. You don't pass up a golden opportunity. I touched the letter from Carol in my back pocket, making sure it was still there.

"I don't know what to tell you. I didn't write all these letters. I wrote maybe one or two after I came to visit the summer right before I married Percy." This had to be Carol.

Standing on tiptoe, I tried to peek into the room. No luck. I hunted around for something to stand on but didn't see anything, so I stood pressed against the side of the RV with my back to the road, listening.

"Aunt Mildred had been so kind to me that summer, and since my own mother wouldn't have anything to do with the wedding, I asked her to come be a part of the celebration."

"I remember that. She went to visit you for a week." Uncle Cyrus's voice softened. "She sure enjoyed helping you with the flowers and picking out the cake. It's all she talked about for months after."

"She was an angel. Even though it was a small service—just friends and family—I couldn't have done it without her." Carol must have moved closer to the window because I could hear her more clearly. "I am sorry for your loss. We heard when we arrived, you'd found her remains. I can't imagine how you must feel."

Cyrus cleared his throat. "Gal, I've known for years that she had passed. There's no way she would've up and left like people were saying."

"It must be a great comfort though, to know for sure. She loved you, Uncle Cyrus. I know because of the way she talked about you. Now, you can lay it to rest. No more wondering."

"No, I can't. I have to find out who did this to her, who took my Mildred from me. Then I can put it to rest."

As I pressed closer to the RV, a hand grabbed my shoulder.

I whipped around, my heart pounding against my ribs, and found myself face-to-face with a teenage boy, maybe sixteen or seventeen. His dyed black hair was slicked back, and an earbud cord dangled across his chest.

"What are you doing?" he asked, his voice breaking on the odd syllable.

"I'm looking for Uncle Cyrus," I said.

"By eavesdropping?"

"No, I ... um ... heard voices and wanted to make sure I was at the right RV."

His brows formed a tight V, and his lips drew into a straight line. "I don't think so. I eavesdrop too often not to know what it looks like." Then concern clouded his face. "You aren't one of dad's friends, are you?"

"I'm looking for Uncle Cyrus. Is he here?"

"You tell me. You're the one listening in on the conversation."

Smart aleck. I decided to take control of the situation, since I refused to be intimidated by an oily-skinned punk. "Look, let's go in and see who's here. Okay?" I used my best 'I'm in charge here' tone. Moving to the stairs, I knocked. The teen followed. I stepped back when the door swung outward, almost tripping over the lanky frame of the boy.

When Carol appeared in the doorway, the teenager tried to start the conversation. "Mom, I found—"

I used my adult status to run roughshod over him. "I

was looking for Uncle Cyrus. Is he here?" I smiled, hoping it radiated charm.

"He's right here. Come on in."

When Carol turned her back to me, I shot the oily punk a heated glare.

He smirked and put his earbud back into his ear. Following close behind me as I climbed the three steps into the RV, he leaned over my shoulder. "Round one goes to you, Princess."

A shiver traveled down my spine, and I batted away his words with my hand.

"Hey, gal, I see you found me." Uncle Cyrus sat on the small couch with his foot propped up on one of the seat cushions.

"I thought you might need some help going back to the party. I'm surprised you guys aren't there."

The teen sauntered over to the kitchenette table and plopped onto the bench seat, holding his phone in his hand.

"You know Amy Kate is one of the best private eyes around."

I shook my head vigorously. "I'm not a private eye. I own a bookshop, The Twisted Plots. Julia might have mentioned it to you."

Carol nodded and took a seat in a swivel chair across from Uncle Cyrus.

"A private eye, huh?" The teen glanced up from his phone. "That explains a lot." He lifted his eyebrows when I made eye contact.

I groaned. "Well, Uncle Cyrus, would you like me to help you back to the reunion?"

"Not really. I'd like to go home. I'm tired, and there are few things I want to look at before tomorrow's Stories of the Family event. I might want to read a few things during it. Will Percy be around tomorrow?" He stood, and I rushed over to keep him from toppling back onto the couch.

Carol shrugged. "I think so. He's participating in the

grill-off. In fact, he left after the picnic luncheon to go buy the meat. He says it's all in the cut."

I grabbed Cyrus's crutches and made sure they were secure under his arms before I let go.

Carol tilted her head back to look up at him. "You know the family story I want to hear, Uncle Cyrus, is the one about your famous pickle jar collection."

"Well, that ain't no story, gal. That's fact. I've been collecting glass jars for as long as I've owned my land out on Dead Man's Curve. My dad taught me never to trust banks. He lost everything in the crash of '29. By the time I came along, he'd started putting his money into what he trusted."

The teen glanced over at Cyrus. I didn't like the gleam of interest I saw in his eyes.

"Come on, Uncle Cyrus. We need to leave if I'm going to get you home and return in time to help Julia with cleanup."

Cyrus took a few wobbly, hop-drag steps toward the door.

"Is it true what they say about those jars?" Carol smiled. "About the money?"

Cyrus laughed, a twinkle in his eye. "Now, gal, who'd put money in a pickle jar?"

A sigh of relief escaped through my lips, and I tried to hide it with my own scoff. "Right, pickle jars. So silly." The letter in my back pocket burned. I didn't want to leave without asking Carol about it, since she'd said she hadn't written the ones Uncle Cyrus had with him. But showing her the letter meant letting Uncle Cyrus know I'd been snooping the other night at his place. But I couldn't pass up this opportunity to talk with Carol away from the rest of her family. I'd have to chance Uncle Cyrus being angry. I pulled the letter out of my pocket. "Carol, I wanted to know, did you write this letter?"

She took the envelope from me and inspected it. "Yes,

this one I remember writing. It's when I invited Aunt Mildred to the wedding. I was telling Uncle Cyrus about it before you got here."

The oily-skinned kid sneered, "She knows."

Confusion washed over Carol's face, but she let the comment pass.

"Where'd you get that, Amy Kate?" Uncle Cyrus's lips tightened, and the heat in his stare could've melted steel.

I squirmed under his glare. "I found it the other night in your edition of *Tom Sawyer*. The illustrations were delightful."

His wrinkles compacted into a scowl, and my gut twisted into a small knot of guilt. "I'm not surprised. Mildred always used whatever was handy for a bookmark, but you shouldn't go through other people's things without their permission."

"You're right." I lifted my hands in surrender. "And I owe you an apology. It's just under the circumstances, I thought it might prove to be useful."

Cyrus nodded. "I suppose. But next time, ask."

Carol handed the letter to Cyrus who added it to the bundle in his hand. He said his good-byes, and I helped him down the three metal steps into the May sunshine.

On our slow walk back to the parking lot, I asked him where he'd found the letters.

"Stuffed in some of Mildred's favorite books, same as you."

"What do they say?"

"Nothing that concerns you. I'm going to handle this. It's family business, so I ought to see to it."

"But it could have something to do with the murder," I pleaded.

"I don't think so. But if I find that it does, I'll let you or the police look at them. Otherwise, I'll handle it." He added a firm nod to his last words. I understood his unspoken message, *hands off*—which, of course, pushed my curiosity into overdrive.

CHAPTER SIX

A blur. It was all a blur. Saturday morning evaporated, and before I knew it, it was time to pick up Uncle Cyrus for the reunion.

The gravel in his driveway crunched under the wheels of my van. I parked close to the porch, so he wouldn't have too far to walk. Before climbing out, I reached down and pushed the front passenger seat back as far as it could go, giving Uncle Cyrus plenty of room for his cast and crutches.

Once on the porch, I cupped my hand around my eyes and peeked through the screen door. I didn't see any movement. It concerned me that Uncle Cyrus had left the front door wide open.

Shaking my head at the man's neglect, I pulled open the screen door and stepped into the front hallway. "Uncle Cyrus, it's me, Amy Kate." I stilled for a moment, listening for his reply. The soft whirl of the ceiling fan in the living room gave me an uneasy feeling. The house was too quiet, and the hairs on the back of my neck prickled.

Then, from somewhere above, the floorboards groaned.

A chill ran down my back. I shook off the

uncomfortable feeling that I'd walked into a horror movie where a masked weirdo, wielding a chainsaw, would pop out at any moment. I took the stairs, a step at a time. I stepped, then listened. I stepped, then listened. Nothing.

Cyrus must be upstairs getting dressed, and if he'd shut the door, he wouldn't have heard me calling. It made sense.

I reached the top landing. "Uncle Cyrus, are you ready? We need to go." For my own comfort, I added, "Everyone will be looking for us."

Not a sound.

I poked my head into his room. The bed was unmade, but a pair of nice tan trousers lay across the pile of crumpled covers.

The bathroom—he must be in the bathroom.

I rapped on the door, waited, but no grumbling voice replied. Then I moved on to the guest room. The door creaked as it followed the slight downhill tilt of the room. Everything appeared to be in order. Where could the man be?

I turned and clomped down the staircase, annoyed that I couldn't find him and even more annoyed that I'd let my imagination run away with me. Open door, creaky floors. I'd watched too many episodes of the *Cold Case True Crime* show with Julia.

Halfway down, a figure in a black hooded jacket shot past the stairs from the library and raced out the screen door. I gasped and clutched at my chest. Then my fright turned to anger.

"Hey," I yelled. "Stop."

I jumped from the third step in an attempt to catch up with the culprit. By the time I reached the porch, a car sped past, coming from the direction of the orchard behind the house. I sprinted off the porch in time to see the license plate. A rental logo caught my eye.

Repeating the letters and the numbers to myself, I raced back to the house's library to write it down before I forgot them. But when I entered the room, I froze.

There, slumped over the desk was Uncle Cyrus. Blood spread over his forehead, and his arms sprawled out in an unnatural pose.

"Uncle Cyrus!" No movement. My heart dropped like a cement block.

I sprinted toward him, leaping over the books that had been flung from the shelves and now littered the floor. Files and papers were scattered everywhere. Rounding the desk, I found the contents of the drawers dumped into small mounds.

He lay still as ice. I reached over his shoulder, placed two fingers on his neck where his pulse should be, and held my breath.

Yes.

Uncle Cyrus was alive.

I snatched my phone out of my pocket and called for help, then tried to wake him, but he didn't response. Afraid to do anything that might make the situation worse, I waited. Within minutes, sirens wailed from the gravel driveway.

Thank goodness for small town traffic.

As soon as the ambulance turned around in the driveway and headed toward the hospital, I called Julia. "I hate to tell you this, but Uncle Cyrus was attacked here at his house."

"What? Oh no, how is he?" Worry filled her voice. "Should I come over?"

"No, I called an ambulance. The paramedics said he'd taken a blow to the head. He's not responding to their attempts to wake him. It would be a good idea if someone from your family went to the hospital. Since there's only so much I could do for him, not being related."

"Yes, of course. Dad will want to go."

"Great. I need to call Gabe now and get him to come

out here and look around. The assailant got away before I could nab him."

"Amy Kate, you could've been hurt." Julia's voice lowered to a heated whisper. "There's a killer on the loose, you know."

"We don't know that for sure, Mildred's killer could be dead or moved away. Besides, I'm fine. Nothing happened. But I surprised him. The library looks like a tornado went through it. He was looking for something—that much is obvious. That's why Gabe should come check it out."

"Okay. Let me go. I don't want Uncle Cyrus to wake up and no one be there."

"All right. Keep me posted."

"Will do. And thanks." The line disconnected.

I went to press Gabe Cooper's number but hesitated with my finger hovering above the button. Glancing around the library, I decided to wait.

Uncle Cyrus was safe and on his way to the hospital, And I'd contacted Julia so someone from the family would meet him there. The rush was over. I flopped into the Queen Anne chair and let out a long sigh. Then my gaze swept the room. What had the culprit been after?

A picture of Uncle Cyrus holding the stack of old letters in his hand popped into my brain. The letters, of course. He'd waved them around at the reunion yesterday to his sister, Emma, his niece Carol, her son, and I'm sure she mentioned them to Percy, her husband—and those were the ones I knew about. No telling who else Carol or the oily teen told about Uncle Cyrus's visit yesterday.

I stood and inched my way along the bookcases, careful not to move anything with my feet.

The books sat topsy-turvy all over one another as if the assailant had opened each one, then tossed it aside when he didn't find what he was looking for. I must've interrupted him before he finished because the books on the bookcase to the right side of the fireplace sat undisturbed.

I knelt and thumbed through a book or two, making sure to replace them as they had been. Something didn't feel right. Uncle Cyrus wouldn't put the letters back into the books; nor would he have left them in the library. I chuckled. Because of me. He knew I couldn't resist seeing what was in them. If he wanted to keep me from finding them, he'd put them somewhere safe, out of sight and inaccessible to me. His room.

I tromped up the stairs taking them two at a time—all thoughts of chain saw-wielding, crazy men left behind.

The sun streamed into the room through the east-facing window. I scanned the area. It held a dresser and mirror, a double-size bed, a chest of drawers, and a bedside table. I did a quick search of the drawers but found nothing.

No. too easy. Think old school. If I were a protective, older man who'd been born after the Depression and grew up during World War II, where would I hide something valuable?

My gaze landed on the unmade bed.

I knelt on the right side of the mattress next to the bedside table and ran my hand under it. Nothing. Moving to the end, I lifted the mattress above the footboard of the bed and pushed my hand as far under it as I could and swept the area. Empty. Finally, I knelt by the left side of the bed and poked my hands under the mattress. There, a few inches from the edge, my hand landed on something. I grabbed it and sank onto the bed.

No letters. Just an old bill for the ring we'd found on the body. The description on the yellow form fit it to a tee. I skimmed through it and flipped the page over to see what was on the back. Nothing.

Stumped, I stood and moved Cyrus's pants to the dresser. Then I ran my hand over the mattress feeling for lumps. Reaching the other side, I found myself now sprawled across the bed, but I decided there might be a better way. I flipped and sat in the middle of the bed at the top and bounced from the headboard to the footboard, hoping I might detect any lumps better with this technique.

"Are you all right?"

My heart jumped into my mouth, and a scream worthy of any Hollywood actress echoed off the walls. I grabbed the paper and hugged it to my chest, scrambling off the bed. Then I saw who it was. "Gabe Cooper, you gave me a heart attack."

"Serves you right. You shouldn't be up here snooping through Cyrus's things. And don't even get me started on the fact you left the front door wide open."

I ignored his admonishment. "What are you doing here?"

"Julia called me. Said her uncle had been attacked out here and wanted to know how the investigation was going. Imagine my surprise to find out you were supposed to call me." His brows wrinkled, forming a jumble of lines on his forehead. "Amy Kate, you can't be here. And yet, here you sit after Cyrus was attacked, and according to Julia, you ran into the assailant. It's dangerous. You need to take this seriously." The nerve near his jawline twitched.

"How is Uncle Cyrus?" I asked to lighten the mood.

Gabe lifted his eyebrows. "Really, you're going to dodge the issue?"

I nodded.

Gabe let out a sigh and moved toward me. "He's alive, and his vitals look all right, but he's not waking up. According to Julia, the doctors said it could be a couple of days up to a few weeks before he comes out of the coma."

"Coma?" The word left a bitter taste in my mouth.

"Yeah, a coma. Lucky for him, he's thick headed, or he'd be dead."

"Do you think they meant to kill him?"

CHAPTER SEVEN

"I'm not sure." Gabe held out his hand. "So, what did you find?"

"Nothing but a receipt for the ring. It's dated 1985, and the description fits the ring we found on the body."

"Yes, it would." Gabe took the piece of paper and scanned it, then laid it on top of the chest of drawers. "Find anything else?"

"No." I shook my head for emphasis.

"Are you sure?" A twinkle of mischief played in his dark brown eyes.

His line of questioning annoyed me, even if he was teasing. I rolled my shoulders and stood to my full five feet two inches. "I don't appreciate your insinuations, Lieutenant Cooper."

"I'm not insinuating anything. You have been known to—let's say—leave a few things out."

"That's only happened once or twice, and the one time, I didn't know the shard of porcelain meant anything." A twinge of guilt pushed me to say, "Besides, you promised not to bring it up again."

Gabe smiled and took me by my shoulders. "I did, didn't I? You're right. I won't bring it up again unless it happens again." His warm eyes swam with amusement, and he dropped his hands. "Are we still on for next weekend? Dinner and a movie?"

I grabbed his hand and gave it a slight squeeze. "Sure are. I'm looking forward to it. It'll be great fun after all this family reunion stuff with Julia. I'll be ready for a night out."

"Hey, anybody here?" Julia's voice floated up the stairs.

"We're up here," Gabe called.

Julia rounded the door jamb. "Hey, y'all. I came to get Uncle Cyrus an overnight bag and some pajamas in case he wakes up. What are you guys doing up here?"

Gabe shifted his gaze to me.

"I was looking for some letters Uncle Cyrus had with him yesterday, but I didn't find them. Thought he might have put them somewhere in his room—" I smiled a half grin at Gabe. "So, I wouldn't find them."

Gabe chuckled. "Umm, letters. What do you know? The first I've heard of them." He nailed me with a hard stare, which told me our previous conversation was not over.

"You mean Uncle Cyrus had others?" Julia's eyes darted to Gabe and back to me. "From you-know-who?"

"Yep. A stack of them, and he showed them to Emma and Carol," I said.

Gabe threw up his hands. "Okay, that's it. Come clean now, and I won't throw you in jail. Date or no date."

"Fine." The bed creaked as I sat on it. "I found a letter to Mildred. It was from Carol inviting Mildred to her wedding to Percy White. Apparently, it was Percy's second marriage, and her mother, Emma, didn't approve. So, Carol asked Mildred to be there for her to help with the preparations for the small ceremony."

"What about the stack of letters that are missing?" Gabe pulled his notebook from his inside coat pocket.

"Who were they from?"

I glanced at Julia. "Those were supposedly also from Carol to Mildred, but—" My gaze moved to Gabe. "When Cyrus asked Carol yesterday if she'd written them, she denied they were from her."

"Interesting." Julia leaned on the bedpost; her thoughts somewhere else.

Gabe scratched a few lines in his notebook. "Who all saw these letters?"

"Emma, Carol, and Carol's youngest son. I don't know his name." I looked to Julia to fill in that information.

"Danny. His name is Danny." Julia stood straight. "Didn't you say the car you saw was a rental?"

"Yes, it was. But don't ask me the license plate number. I caught a glimpse of it as the car passed me coming from the orchard, and I ran into the library to write it down, but when I found Uncle Cyrus, I panicked and forgot all about it." I glanced toward Gabe and shrugged. "Sorry."

"So, a car came from around the back of the house from the orchard?"

"Right, as I was coming down the stairs, someone in a hooded jacket ran through the downstairs hallway and out the front door. I followed, and by the time I reached the porch steps, the car whizzed by throwing gravel."

"Did you see which way it turned at the end of the drive?" Gabe asked.

"No, I didn't notice. I was too busy trying to remember the stupid license plate number." I said, disgruntled.

Gabe wrote one or two more things on his paper and then tucked the notebook back into his suitcoat pocket. "It's a good thing it rained last night. Let's go look out back. See if we can figure out where the car had been waiting. It might give us an idea if there were one or two assailants."

"Two assailants?" Julia asked.

"Yeah, one to find whatever they were looking for and

one to drive the car."

We followed the tire tracks in the mud around the house to the back. The further we went, the more obvious it became that the car had been parked next to the orchard. The footprints in the muddy area squished together to the point of being obscure. In the orchard, we discovered several holes under the apple trees, scattered here and there near where the tire tracks ended. Two shovels lay discarded.

Gabe walked over to the shovel nearest him while Julia and I waited on the edge of the row of apple trees where the holes seemed to start. Reaching into his front suit pocket, he pulled out a handkerchief and bent over, picked up the spade, and inspected it. Then carefully, he laid it back down by the hole where he found it and crossed over the ground to the second shovel. He didn't lift this one. Instead, he squatted and inspected the metal end without moving it. "There's blood on this one."

Julia and I exchanged looks.

"Do you think this is where the attack happened?" Julia wrung her hands.

"I'll need to look over the library to see if there are any signs of blood other than where you found him. But yes, this might be the place where he was attacked."

Julia and I moved toward Gabe. "There are little holes in the mud by the footprints that could be from Cyrus's crutches, but how did he get into the library to his desk?" I stood over the hole where the second shovel sat. Blood colored the back of the shovel a dark crimson. Gabe was right. Cyrus was lucky to be alive.

Julia pressed her lips together and shook her head. "Why would someone dig up Uncle Cyrus's orchard?"

"Maybe because of the crazy story about the pickle jars." Gabe looked up at Julia who stood opposite him. "From the looks of things, someone believes that cockamamy story."

"But anyone who knows Uncle Cyrus would know that tale has been floating around for decades. Shoot, it probably started with Great-grandpa Ernest and attached to Uncle Cyrus because of his penchant for glass jars." Julia hugged her middle.

I wrapped an arm around my friend to steady her. "Well, he does enjoy teasing people with his tale of buried treasure in the orchard. Think he likes to see everyone's reaction."

Gabe's attention turned to the hole.

"Yes, but he always makes sure they know he's just teasing. That there's no truth to it," Julia said.

"Are you sure there's no truth to it?" Gabe placed one knee on the soggy grass and plunged his hand into the hole. With some effort, he wiggled the item in his grasp free from the dirt, lifting it for us to see. The metal ring on the glass jar glistened in the hot May sun like diamonds, but the hundred-dollar bills that were stuffed to its rim shone with the power of enlightenment.

Not only was Uncle Cyrus's crazy tale of burying money in his orchard true, but the assailants now knew it.

Gabe stood, holding the jar. "This isn't good."

"No," I echoed his sentiment. "It's not."

Julia shook her head, wide eyed. "I would've never believed it in a million years."

"We can't let anyone know," Gabe said. "If people find out there's money out here, they'll mob the place. As it is, we'll have to have men watching the area around the clock. I'll have a patrol car cruise by hourly 'cause you can bet your money-filled jars those guys who were here today will be back to finish the job."

CHAPTER EIGHT

Julia and I stood in the driveway next to her car.

"I am so sorry about your Uncle Cyrus." My heart ached for my friend. Her parents were as worried as she was about the dear old man. And yet they still had a family reunion to host.

"I can't believe any of this. In just a few days, Uncle Cyrus is in a coma, and there's oodles of money in the orchard, and Aunt Mildred's remains were found in a pothole. I'm stunned." She leaned against the passenger side door, her shoulders sagging. "I've had more skeletons pop out of my family closet in the last week than I've come across in my entire life." She raised her eyes and met my gaze.

"Is there anything I can do?" The words sounded so glib. "I can sit with Cyrus tonight, while you're dealing with the reunion."

"No, Dad and Mom and I are going to take shifts over the next few days. Then we'll see what needs to be done." Julia paused. "But you can do one thing for me."

"Name it." Julia and I had been best friends since junior high school. I'd walk on nails for her.

"Catch the culprit who did this to Uncle Cyrus."

I flinched. Gabe warned me not to continue looking into this matter. He'd made himself crystal clear I was to leave it alone, right before the patrol car showed up and parked on the edge of the driveway to guard the property. He was pretty sure whoever had started this would be back.

Julia read my hesitation. "Look, Gabe and the Pine Lake Police Department are some of the finest law enforcement officers around, but they're not you. You know this town, you know the people, and you know Uncle Cyrus. I'm afraid if you don't help, he'll end up in prison for Mildred's murder or worse."

She was right about the possibility of Cyrus being charged with Mildred's murder. Even Gabe had said nine times out of ten it was the spouse. With that thinking, Cyrus didn't stand a chance. Yet, Gabe had told me not to get mixed up in it. He had a bad feeling it wasn't going to end well. And he couldn't catch the killer if he had to worry about me, too.

I pressed my lips together, but Julia's expectant eyes got to me. I couldn't and wouldn't let Julia down. "Of course, I'll find him. And when I do, I'll make sure he gets everything he deserves." I offered a half smile while a knot the size of Texas formed in my gut.

I only hoped I wasn't promising more than I could deliver.

As I pulled to the end of the gravel driveway, I noticed the road construction crew down Crestwood Road on the left-hand side. A thought drifted into my mind as I watched them working. Instead of turning right, I turned left, pulled up alongside the men, and rolled down my window. "Excuse me," I hollered over the roar of the machinery.

A young man in an orange vest holding a sign with the word *Slow* on one side and *Stop* on the other walked toward me. "Ma'am, you can't stop here."

"But I have a question." I blinked my lashes

innocently.

He frowned. "What's the question?"

"How long have you been working here today? I mean, what time did you start?"

"We've been here since seven this morning. Why?" He propped his arm on top of my roof and leaned down into my window.

"Well," I started to say the house up the road had been robbed, but I didn't want to have to answer the questions that might bring up. But I didn't want to tell a lie either. After all, I'm a good Christian girl. Most of the time. So instead, I said, "Someone, a stranger, was seen at the house up the road."

"You mean the one where we found the body?"

"Yeah, that one." So much for being discreet. "And I wondered if you'd seen a black compact car zip past here—say around ten o'clock?"

The young man puckered his lips, squinted his eyes, and looked off into the distance. Slowly, he shook his head. "Nope, I can't say I saw a black compact."

"Oh," I said, "Well, thank—".

"But I do recall seeing a blue pickup truck pulling out of the drive right before nine." He grinned. "I hadn't noticed it going in 'cause I was on the other side of the equipment. We had a backed-up situation. The cars were six deep. But later, I saw the truck pull out and head in our direction."

My heart picked up speed. "Did you happen to get a look at the driver."

"Oh yeah, he was an older man maybe in his sixties, gray hair, and a weird-looking mole on his cheek. That's why I remember him. Big ole thing." He laughed. "At first, I thought it was a bug—"

A honk behind me saved me from the story.

"You'll need to move along now, miss. A pleasure speaking with you."

The young man patted the roof of my car and then pushed himself to a standing position and flipped his sign to the side that read *Stop*. "You go on now. I'll hold them back so you can pass without any trouble." He flashed me a wide smile, before I continued down the road.

My mind whirled with questions. Could the man in the blue truck be Mildred's old flame, Gary Martin? And if so, what in heaven's name was he doing at Uncle Cyrus's house this morning? Did he have anything to do with the ransacking of the library? Could he be the second assailant?

I couldn't force my mind to focus. There were too many what ifs and not enough facts. I needed to think, to sort it out, and the person I normally did that with was the one person I couldn't ask to do it. Julia. This time she was too close. I'd have to find someone else to help me sort through it, but who?

CHAPTER NINE

The smell of meat grilling wafted through the hot afternoon air. There were about ten of the fifty or so aunts, uncles, and cousins at the reunion, participating in the family grill-off event. The grills sat clustered together in the park a few feet apart from one another, not far from the lunch tent.

I moved toward the grilling area. The fact Cyrus had said yesterday that the letters pertained to family business led me to think our assailant was part of the reunion.

The grill-off started at noon, so if one of Julia's relatives had been the guy I met at Cyrus's house, he'd have barely made it back in time. I wanted to see if anyone seemed out of sorts, Percy White, in particular.

I hadn't met Percy yet, and since Uncle Cyrus was anxious to see him yesterday, I wanted to make his acquaintance. Plus, Uncle Cyrus had talked about the money jars in front of Danny and Carol. The gleam in Danny's eyes when Cyrus mentioned them had made me uneasy. It wasn't too big of a leap to think they'd told Percy about the local lore.

It didn't take me long to pick him out from the other grill-off competitors. Julia had described him as an older version of the teenage son. Sure enough, he stood next to the grill, dyed black hair, forty pounds overweight, wearing a Hawaiian shirt which read 'squeeze me, please' above the pocket.

Every fiber in my being yelled "run away!"

But I had no choice. Julia asked me to find the person who had done this to Cyrus, and for her, my best friend, I'd deal with as many sleazy, uncouth, potential killers as necessary to find the truth.

I moved toward Percy's grill, stopping along the way to compliment some of the other contestants. I didn't want it to be too obvious that I was here to see him.

Carol sat in one of the lawn chairs among a ring of them a few feet away, chatting with Betsy and Jim. She laughed at something and swatted in Betsy's direction.

"Smells good." I sidled up to the grill.

"Thank you very much." Percy White hummed as he turned to grab a bowl of sauce from the folding table next to the grill. "It's an old favorite that I added a little kick to. To ensure I win."

"What's the prize?" I asked.

"Two hundred dollars, and of course, bragging rights." He chuckled.

I nodded and plastered a smile on my face. "Who couldn't use some extra cash?"

Percy's eyebrows winged up. "Right. Nothing like free money."

"Well, don't you have to win the competition first?" I asked.

"Oh yeah, but—" he leaned in close to me. "It's like taking candy from a baby. None of these folks know the first thing about grilling. It's obvious. Look over there."

I turned in the direction he nodded. A thirty-something man stood fanning black smoke away from his grill. The frown on his face made it clear something was on fire besides his coals.

A few feet in the other direction, two women worked on cutting their meat to the perfect thickness. Except they couldn't agree what that thickness should be. One of the women wore all white which showed a great deal of confidence for a grilling event. The one holding the knife pointed at the other one in the white shirt. For a moment, I thought I'd need to step in, but the knife wielder turned back to her meat that lay on the stainless-steel cart parked beside her grill. The one in the white shirt leaned over her, pointing and shaking her head.

"I see what you mean." I hated to agree with the man.

He finished slathering the sauce over the meat and closed the lid. Glancing at his watch, he punched a button, then tsked. "You got to catch it at the right time. Too long and it's tough as shoe leather, not long enough and it looks like an Egyptian sacrifice. Who wants to eat that?" His brows furrowed, recognition dawning in his eyes. "Hey, you're Julia's friend, aren't you?" He asked, pointing his finger at me. "The one who came by the R.V. yesterday to help Uncle Cyrus?"

"Guilty." I couldn't help looking at his hand and noticing the red stain under his soiled fingernails as if he'd been digging in wet red clay dirt.

"Yeah, Carol and Danny mentioned you when they told me Cyrus had been looking for me." He followed my gaze and stuffed his hands into the pockets of his Bermuda shorts. "Well, nice to meet you. I'd better go see if Carol needs me while I have a few minutes. See ya." He pivoted in his flip-flops and made a beeline for Carol.

So, they had discussed Cyrus's visit. I glanced his way. He was leaning in close to Danny, the oily teenager. They both caught me staring.

Scanning the crowd, I looked for Julia, but instead, I spotted Gabe. He smiled when his gaze met mine and started toward me. I headed in his direction, and we met somewhere near the tent. "Hey, what are you doing here?" I asked.

"I could ask you the same thing." He paused. "But I won't. I have a feeling I know what brought you here. I suppose I should give up on the idea that you'll stay out of this and let me handle it."

"Probably." I shrugged. "You know me, Gabe. I can't stand by and watch. Not when it's someone I care about."

The warmth in his sweet brown eyes added to my guilt. I hated being torn. "Look, I know it's not much, but Percy White, Carol's husband, has red stains under his fingernails."

"Huh. Did you get a chance to look at the kid's hands?" Gabe asked.

"No, not yet." It took a second for his words to register. "Wait. What did you say?"

"If you're going to be looking into this matter, I might as well enlist your help. At least that way, I'll know where you are and what you're up to."

"So, you're saying you're going to let me help?" I pressed my lips together to keep from squealing with delight. I hated the circumstances, but at least now, I didn't have to sneak around to help Julia and Uncle Cyrus.

"Can I stop you?" Gabe lifted both shoulders and his eyebrows in one motion.

Reaching out, he pushed a piece of my blonde hair back behind my ear and let his finger brush across my cheek. "I just want you safe. This way I can keep an eye on you. But you are not to go nosing around alone again like today. I want you to keep me or Elizabeth updated on your whereabouts. Understood?" He stepped closer and placed his hands on my shoulders. "Safety first, Amy Kate. I'd like to have our date next Saturday night as planned."

His eyes held mine. I wanted to dispel the concern I saw in them. But there wasn't much I could do to reassure him. "Well, then if we're working together, guess I'd better tell you what I found out from one of the men on the road construction crew."

Gabe cocked his head to one side, looking adorable, and a half grin played on his lips. "I'm listening."

My concentration failed me. "I ...umm ... I discovered ..." I took a step back so I could think. "I discovered one of the crew saw a blue pickup pulling out of the driveway around nine o'clock this morning. The guy got a good look at the driver. From the description, it could be Gary Martin."

"Mildred's high school sweetheart?" Gabe asked. "Why would he be at Cyrus's house?"

I shook my head. "I'm not sure. Every time I figure out what's going on, something else pops up leading in a different direction." A thought struck me. "When do you get off duty?"

Gabe's smile spread across his face and raced to his eyes. "Around six. What do you have in mind?"

"How does Chinese sound? I'll pick up some shrimp lo mein from Mr. Wrong's Place and meet you at Twisted Plots. We can go over what we know so far. And I can pay off my oatmeal raisin cookie debt."

"Homemade?" Gabe asked.

"Is there any other kind?"

"Okay, sounds great. Maybe we can untangle a few details. Get a better handle on which direction to go. I'll see if Floyd can come too."

"Is that necessary?" I hadn't counted on it being anyone but us. The whole point was to work through the facts. Too many people, and all we'd wind up with would be opinions.

"He's my partner. I'd like to keep him informed. Besides, I wouldn't want him becoming jealous." Gabe winked at me, and I caved.

"Fine, I'll order enough for three."

"Better make it four. If my dad's working tonight at the bookshop, he'll want an egg roll or two as well."

Great. There goes my attempt to untangle this mess.

CHAPTER TEN

Carter dashed to the glass door to open it when he spotted me on the sidewalk with my arms full. Gabe looked a lot like his father, handsome, a firm square jawline, but it was their personalities that were so similar. Both were kindhearted, smart, and had a strong sense of justice. Best of all, both were loyal to a fault. It's what made Gabe a great detective. It's what made Carter Cooper a wonderful employee and friend.

"I see you brought Chinese, and do I smell cookies?" Carter grinned.

"Yes, fresh from the oven, sort of."

"And enough food for the whole Chinese army. I can't handle all this myself."

I giggled. "We're expecting company."

"Oh, we are?" Carter released the door and followed me to the back room. A customer sat in one of the club chairs near the floor-length window, and a few milled around in the mystery section.

I nodded to Kyle, the college student who worked nights and weekends, as I passed the counter and hurried down the short hall to the workroom, glad I'd remembered to order enough for him, too.

"Here, let me help." Carter pulled the top bag of food from my arms.

I set the other two bags on the worktable that stood chest-high and pushed the two sleek computers used to log in inventory to one end of the eight-foot surface. The cookies in a plastic bag, I tossed in the center.

"I brought some for you, Kyle, Gabe, Floyd, and me."

"Sounds like a party. Maybe I ought to call Maureen and get her down here." He chuckled.

I raised my hands, palms out. "No, please. I love Maureen, but this was supposed to be a meeting of the minds, but now it's more like a collision of the cosmos."

Carter nodded his understanding. "I'll get the plates and forks. Did you remember the chopsticks?"

"I sure did." I pulled them from the bag.

"Something smells delicious." Gabe entered the workroom, and two seconds later Floyd Simms, his partner, followed.

"Hi, Amy Kate. Thanks for letting me tag along." Floyd looked to be in his mid-forties, and the slight paunch that hung over his belt spoke of the many sedentary hours he spent behind a desk or on a stakeout. He walked over to one of the swivel stools covered in the blue china pattern and hoisted himself onto it. "I have to admit I could eat."

Carter handed him a plate, and I finished unloading the bags. Once Carter went up front, Kyle stepped in to fill his plate and managed to snag the last egg roll.

Once everyone finished their meal, I closed the containers and stored the leftovers in the mini fridge while Gabe threw away the plates and bags.

"All right gentlemen, let's get down to business." I took my seat.

Usually with Julia all this unraveling of facts and people came naturally. We didn't need all this formality—we simply discussed what we knew. But with these two, I wasn't sure what to expect. How I missed Julia.

I checked my watch. She'd be finishing up the family bingo session in the tent and preparing to serve the meats from the grill-off as part of the dinner. Later this evening, a softball game and fireworks were planned as the grand finale to the Jacobs' family reunion. The cherry on top, as Julia said.

Gabe cleared his throat and brought me back to the task at hand. "So, what are you thinking? What stands out the most to you?"

"The first point we need to consider is who knew about the jars buried in the orchard." I glanced at Floyd to see what he thought.

"I agree," he said. "Who knew about them? And why now?"

"Yes, I hadn't thought about that. Why now?" Energy surged through me. I needed a pen and paper to write this down—get it all out of my head and see it in black and white. Sliding off my seat, I went to my desk and grabbed a few sheets of paper and a pen. "So, who knew?"

Gabe groaned and leaned against the back of his stool. "Everyone in Pine Lake. He's been going around for years telling the tale of his buried pickle jars, just to see how people would react."

Floyd nodded.

I sighed and wrote the word 'everyone' on my paper. Not a great start.

"What about Floyd's question? Why now?" I asked.

"My gut tells me it goes back to the reunion." Gabe frowned. "That's why I told Julia to make an announcement asking everyone to remain in Pine Lake. It makes sense."

"I agree," I said. "Anyone else in town could've gone to Cyrus's house at any time to check out his story. The reunion is now, and that's why this has happened now. From the way Danny White reacted to Uncle Cyrus's story, I'd lay odds it was the first time he'd ever heard about the pickle jars."

"And digging up the orchard sounds like something a teenager might attempt," Floyd added.

"True." Gabe leaned forward and put his elbows on the worktable.

"And Julia did say this was the first time in years Carol and her family have attended. So, they wouldn't have heard Cyrus's tale before." I looked across the table at Gabe. "Did you ever get a chance to look at Danny's hands?"

Floyd furrowed his brow. "His hands?'

"Yeah, his father, Percy White, had red stained fingernails today at the grill-off like he'd been digging in red-clay dirt. I had to leave to come back to the bookshop before I had a chance to check Danny's."

Gabe smiled. "I got a look at his hands at lunch. I made a point to sit at his table in the tent so I could be there when Julia made the announcement."

"And?" I asked, bursting with anticipation.

"Red, just like his dad's."

"Well, there it is. Now, you can go arrest them." I leaned my elbow on the table and placed my chin in the palm of my hand, satisfied we had a firm case.

"We can't arrest anyone. Dirty, red fingernails are not enough to convict on assault and attempted murder." Gabe said. "But I wish it were."

"What about the letters?" Floyd asked. I could see why Gabe wanted to bring him. He asked the right questions.

"The letters are another part of all this," Gabe stated.

"I don't see how the letters have anything to do with the attack on Cyrus, but they must, or they wouldn't be missing." I leaned back in my chair and crossed my arms. "How are the letters connected?" I mumbled under my breath.

Gabe tapped the table. "Let's make a list of the possible suspects from the reunion who knew about the letters." Gabe ticked them off on his fingers. "First we have

Carol, then Percy, and Danny."

"And their Great-aunt Emma. Cyrus talked with her about the letters as well." I added her name to the list. "Plus, we don't know who they might have told."

"True." Floyd rubbed his chin, then grabbed his takeout cup from Wrong's Place and took a long drink. "Here's another thought." He set the cup back on the worktable. "How did they know where to dig?"

Floyd was hitting it out of the park.

I slid off the stool and started to pace. "So, we have a library that's trashed, books pulled off the shelves and discarded in piles, holes in the orchard with jars scattered here and there, missing letters, and a man in a coma." I looked at Gabe and Floyd.

"That about sums it up," Floyd said.

"But what does that tell us?" My mind jumped between the facts. How did they all fit together. "What do you think the sequence of events were?"

Gabe shrugged. "Cyrus was home, maybe in the library or the orchard."

"Or in his bedroom. His dress pants were out on the bed for him to change into before the reunion," I said.

"Okay, let's say he's in the bedroom, getting ready. He hears someone drive onto the property. When no one comes to the house, he goes looking for him. He finds him in the orchard, digging holes, looking for his money."

Floyd jumped in. "Cyrus threatens him and goes to call the cops. The assailant knocks him out before he goes too far, then pulls the books from the shelves to make it look like someone broke into the house."

"Well, we know for sure he was hurt in the orchard because of the blood on the shovel and then moved to the library—no matter what order the other events happened in. So that tells us a lot."

I squinted. "What does it tell us?"

"There were two assailants. Uncle Cyrus isn't a small

man. Even for his age and with that cast on his right leg, he'd be hard to move. No, there had to be at least two people in the orchard."

Floyd nodded. "That makes sense. Two people would've been able to carry Cyrus to the library, but it's a long distance to cover alone."

"Right." Now, Gabe stood. "So, we have two assailants. We also know another important fact."

"I'll play along. What's that?" Floyd grinned.

"They didn't intend to kill Cyrus. They're not murderers. If they'd wanted him dead, they had every opportunity after they knocked him out to finish the job. I mean they had time to drag him to the library and pose him, so we'd think it had happened there, that it was a break-in."

"Why would they want you to think it happened in the library?" I asked.

"So we wouldn't look in the orchard and find out Cyrus's story was true. Maybe they thought they'd have another chance to dig up some more of those jars." Floyd leaned back and smacked his lips before picking up his cup for another drink of sweet tea.

Gabe's smile spread across his cheeks exposing his dimples. "And it might have worked if you hadn't come along. When you showed up, the driver had to give away their secret to keep his partner from being caught."

The heat of embarrassment crept up my neck and blossomed on my face. "I blame my trouble magnet. It keeps me in the wrong place at the wrong time."

Floyd shook his foam cup, and the ice swished against the sides. "I hope I grow up to be like you." He chuckled.

Gabe became quiet. "Now, all we have to do is figure out how they knew where to dig because there were jars beside all the holes. And where did the letters go?"

"Well," I said, "don't most buried treasures have a map?"

Floyd's lips curled into a smile, causing his face to

widen. "I do believe the fair maiden is correct."

"Yes, but what kind of map would a man like Cyrus make? Trust me. It won't have an X marking all the spots. If he didn't trust banks, he sure wasn't going to make his cash easy to find."

Gabe had a point. Cyrus must have a map somewhere, but if the assailants already had it, there was no point in us looking for it because I couldn't imagine Cyrus making a copy. No. There was only one.

Squaring my shoulders, I said, "How about we divide up the list of names?"

"Okay, but if you find anything, you report back to me immediately." Gabe frowned. "Remember, we're a team."

"Aye, aye, mon Lieutenant." I saluted. "I'll talk with Carol and Emma and leave those dirty fingernailed gents to you guys."

"Sounds good." Floyd slid off the stool and sauntered over to the trash can beside my desk, chucking in the cup. The takeout bags crunched when it landed. "I'm gonna head out. Let me know if you two find anything." He continued out the door and down the hall.

"Yeah, I'd better go too. Now that I know I'm looking for two assailants, I might go talk with Percy and Danny tonight." Gabe stopped in front of me and placed his hands on my shoulders. "Be safe out there. Don't do anything rash." He cocked his head to one side. The movement sort of reminded me of Gizmo, my Scottish terrier.

"You know me. I'm never rash." But there was no way I was making him any other promises. No, I had a rat or two to catch. And I'd do whatever it took to get them to squeak. I gathered the trash bag and tied it tight, lugging it out back to the dumpster. Swinging the bag up and over the blue rim, I let the black lid clank shut. I half expected Uncle Cyrus to appear like he had so many nights before—but not tonight. Tonight, he lay unconscious in the hospital, depending on me to find the people who put him there.

CHAPTER ELEVEN

On Sundays, Elizabeth and I met Dad and our sister, Alexia, her husband, Cole, and their son, Grant, in the third pew to the left of the middle aisle at First Community Church. Today, Julia joined us.

Dad had taken to having us all over for a nice big family dinner afterwards. It helped him keep connected. Since his retirement from the police department, he'd been trying to spend more time with us.

Today, chicken and dumplings topped the menu. I needed a good dose of comfort food.

He stood over the stove stirring so the dumplings wouldn't stick together as I pinched off pieces of the canned biscuit dough and dropped them into the hot broth.

"My stomach is growling. I could eat a small dinosaur."

Dad chuckled. "You've always had a good appetite." He pushed the dumplings apart and made a space for me to drop in the next one. "I'm glad you invited Julia. She looks worn out."

"Her family reunion was more work and less play than she'd bargained for, and then everything with her Uncle Cyrus." I shook my head and dropped in another dumpling.

"I can understand her concern." He sighed, then pressed his lips together before saying, "I know it's none of my business—"

I cut my eyes toward him and stepped back from the pot. "Go on."

"I ran into Carter this morning, and he told me you and Gabe and Floyd had a meeting last night in your back workroom. That wouldn't have anything to do with the attack on Cyrus, would it?"

I stared down at my hands holding the dough. "Um. Yes, in a way. We were going over certain facts about the assault. Gabe let me sit in since I was the eyewitness."

Dad's brows furrowed into a tight V. That didn't bode well for me.

My father is the quintessential dad, overprotective of his girls. Add in the fact he used to be a homicide detective, and you have a bulldog on steroids.

"I don't want you getting mixed-up in this thing. It's bad enough they found Mildred's body, but then Cyrus is attacked. I talked with Julia's dad yesterday. He says they don't know when Cyrus will wake up."

"I know."

"That could've been you." His lips tightened into a straight line. A wave of worry crossed his face.

"But Julia asked me to help, and I can't let her down," I said.

He stirred the broth. "Let Gabe handle it. He's a fine detective."

"I know. He learned from the best." I grinned at him and gave a little wink.

He shook his head and groaned. "Flattery will get you nowhere, but I can see by the look on your face I'm wasting my breath."

I shrugged. "So, what do you know about the case?"

"Mildred's disappearance?" He turned toward the pot and gave the broth a good long stir. "I know Cyrus didn't do it." He tapped the spoon on the rim of the pot.

"What makes you say that? I mean I don't think he did either, or I wouldn't be helping to find the person who *did* do this to Mildred."

Dad pointed the spoon at me. "I knew you were neck deep in this." Then he placed it in the ceramic spoon holder on the counter. "We never could find any proof of foul play. No weapon, no blood stains, nothing which lead us to believe she hadn't left. Add in the suitcase and clothes gone—" Dad shook his head. "It didn't add up to Cyrus killing her."

"Couldn't he have packed it after the fact, to make his story plausible?" I asked.

"Yes." Dad stopped and met my gaze. "But most killers aren't that thorough. They forget the little details like her favorite ring or the hairbrush. All those items were gone. As if she'd packed the suitcase herself and left."

I leaned my hip against the edge of the cabinet.

"I was wrong about there being a murder." His eyebrows winged up. "So, you, young lady, be careful."

"I will. And besides, Gabe's got my back."

Dad smiled. "He's a good man. I hope you know I approve of him if you were to ever ... you know ... think about settling down."

"Dad, you're acting like an old Italian mother. Cooking and dispensing love advice." But I couldn't help the warm flutter that rippled through me at the thought of all the possibilities that the future held.

Alexia entered the kitchen holding baby Grant with Julia close behind her, making faces at the little tyke over Alexia's shoulder. His feet never touched the floor when he was with us.

Dad handed Alexia the spoon and took Grant from her arms. He held the baby close to his chest and slowly twirled around the kitchen.

A squeal rang out, then little bubbles of laughter

floated from him. His full cheeks and blond curls made him irresistible. As Dad twirled, Grant leaned his head back, putting all his weight on the arms that held him.

Julia grinned. "I wish I could be so trusting. Look, he doesn't have a care in the world."

I smiled, catching the joy that leaked from the baby. "I know. Wouldn't it be wonderful?"

"Yes, it would." Julia sighed.

I didn't like seeing my optimistic friend stressed out. It didn't suit her. Nothing like a murder and violent attacks to bring down a family reunion. She'd worked so hard on it, too. What a shame.

Alexia dipped the spoon into the pot and pushed the dumplings out of the way.

Turning my attention back to the meal, I dropped the last three balls of dough into the simmering broth.

About then, the front door banged shut. Alexia laid the spoon on the counter and turned toward the sound.

"Something smells good in here," Elizabeth called out before she appeared in the kitchen doorway.

"We've been slaving away while you were off playing." Dad chuckled.

"How is your client?" I asked.

"Stable but not awake." Elizabeth looked toward Julia, and I followed her gaze.

Julia stood by the island, pressing her lips together.

Elizabeth took a carrot off the veggie tray Alexia had brought and dipped it in the ranch dressing. Before taking a bite, she said, "Don't worry, Julia. He's a fighter. He'll wake up. No reason not to think he won't."

"I know. It's just this whole mess with the family. First the skeleton and now this. Someone hurt Uncle Cyrus, and I can't help thinking the two things are connected. The attack on Uncle Cyrus must be connected to the reunion. I feel like it's my fault. I knew finding Mildred had upset him. I should've kept a better eye on him."

"It's not your fault." I patted her shoulder. "Cyrus Jacobs does what Cyrus Jacobs wants to. That's all there is to it. Muleheaded, according to Flora."

"I know, but I feel like I could've done more. When I saw him with those letters, I should've intervened," Julia said.

"What letters?" Elizabeth leaned toward Grant and tickled his tummy.

"Cyrus showed up at the reunion Friday with a stack of letters. I found one tucked away in a book in his library the week before when I was there helping with his broken foot," I said.

Elizabeth's brow crinkled into lines. "What did they say?"

"I'm not sure. I only read the one. It was from Carol White. Well, Carol Jacobs at the time. She'd written it the summer before her wedding." I turned my attention to Julia. "Besides, you couldn't know that Cyrus would go fishing around with those letters. This isn't your fault."

"You're right. It's like this whole reunion has been doomed from the beginning." Julia's head drooped.

"So, what did the letter say?"

My sister the pit bull. Once Elizabeth got ahold of something, she worked it until she had everything she needed. It made her a great lawyer.

"The one I read asked Mildred to come to her wedding ceremony. It hinted that Carol's mother, Emma, wasn't too keen on the marriage, since it was Percy's second."

"Hm, interesting." Elizabeth studied me. "Anything else?"

I picked up the spoon from the counter and stirred the chicken and dumplings.

"Anything else?" Elizabeth repeated.

I glanced toward her. "If you must know, they're missing."

"What do you mean missing?"

"Well, you know about the dug-up jars in the orchard. And I suppose you know they ransacked the library where they left Cyrus to be found. I'm guessing to make it look like a robbery and to keep the police from looking in the orchard."

"Yeah, Gabe told me about that," Elizabeth said.

"When I found the library in a wreck, I figured they might have been looking for the letters. Several people at the reunion saw him with them, and he'd confronted some of them about the letters. So, after I'd called Julia and the ambulance, I searched for them."

"Did you find them?" Julia asked.

"No, and Friday when I drove Cyrus home from the reunion, he took the letter that I had. So, all the letters are gone."

Dad shook his head. "Tough break. Maybe they could've given Gabe a clue as to what this is all about."

"That's what I'm thinking. But I don't plan to give up the search. They have to be somewhere." The minute I left dad's, I planned to go over to the R.V. park to talk to Carol. She'd seen the letters. Maybe she could shed some light on their contents.

Elizabeth grabbed another carrot from the tray. "That is, if they're still intact. Someone might have taken them to destroy them, if they thought they were connected to Mildred's murder."

CHAPTER TWELVE

My mind whirled as I merged onto the highway. Leave it to my sister, Elizabeth, to point out the dark clouds. What if she were right and the letters had been destroyed?

I couldn't shake the feeling that the letters were the key to what had happened to Cyrus. And maybe, even Mildred. Then there was the map, if it even existed. Only Cyrus knew and he wasn't talking. I swallowed the lump burning in my throat.

A few minutes later, I pulled into the parking lot of the Pine Lake Campgrounds. I recognized some of Julia's relations coming from the hiking trail that wound around the lake. Unbuckling my seatbelt, I stepped out of the van. Carol wasn't anywhere around, but Danny and Percy stood over by a stack of canoes hosing one off.

Good, she'd be alone.

When Gabe and Floyd and I had divided up the list of suspects, I'd asked for her name. Well, hers and Great-aunt Emma. The mere thought of the older woman filled me with dread.

The gate to the R.V. section of the campgrounds stood open. I thought about driving to Carol's R.V. site, since it would be faster but decided against it. The walk would do me good and give me time to think of a way to broach the subject. I didn't think the direct approach of asking her if she stole the letters would be considered couth.

By the time I reached the R.V., I had a plan. I rapped on the metal door and waited. Footsteps echoed in the small space.

"Coming," called a female voice.

The door swung out and revealed Carol White in a pink robe with her hair wrapped in a towel.

"Oh, I'm sorry. I didn't mean to get you out of the shower." The heat of embarrassment crept up the back of my neck.

"No, it's fine. We went canoeing earlier, and I'm just now getting around to cleaning up." Carol stepped back and swept her arm toward the couch. "Won't you come in?"

I stepped up the three small metal stairs and crossed to the couch. Sitting down, I waited for Carol to close the door.

She turned and greeted me with a smile. "Can I offer you a soda or water?"

"No but thank you." I ran the palms of my hands down the tops of my jeans, unsure how to start this conversation.

Carol stood waiting.

"I came to offer you our couch in case you guys need it. You weren't expecting to be here this long, and with such tight quarters …" I shrugged and let her fill in the blanks however she wanted.

"Oh, how sweet," she gushed. "Julia's always told me how kind you are, but now I know it for myself." Her smile widened, and she sat in the chair opposite me, pulling her robe tight around her legs. The towel on her head drooped a little to the left. "But I couldn't impose."

"Well, I know how difficult it can be. A whole family jammed into a small space."

"Tell me about it. Danny is about to go stir crazy. If I

hear, 'I'm bored,' one more time, I'll let the bears have him." A glint came into her eyes. "You know on second thought—"

Uh oh. What had I done? She'd already declined. Isn't there a rule about no backsies?

"I think I will take you up on your offer. It'd be nice if Danny could see more of Pine Lake besides the campgrounds, and you and Julia live near the town square, don't you?"

"Yeah." I nodded my head as the rest of my body went numb. I didn't want to have to deal with a snarky teenager.

When I worked out the plan in my head, she'd declined the invitation, stating they had beds here. I thought it to be a safe, surefire, 'thanks but no thanks.' Why is it that ideas always sound better in your head than they do coming from your lips?

"Well, that's about perfect. He can walk to town and entertain himself. I do believe you are my hero." Carol beamed.

I plastered on a tight-lipped smile and nodded my assent.

Well, if Julia and I were stuck with an oily, smart-aleck, house guest for the next few days, I intended to get the information I needed. "I also wanted to ask you about Uncle Cyrus's visit the other day."

"Yes, that was odd, wasn't it?"

"I'm interested in those letters." I leaned back against the couch to let her know that I'd no intentions of leaving anytime soon.

"It was strange. To see my name signed to those letters and to know I hadn't written them. Of course, I wrote a few but not the amount Uncle Cyrus showed me. I kind of know now how people feel when their identities are stolen. It's creepy." Her face squished into a pucker of disdain.

"Did you have a chance to read any of them?"

"I did. One of them was dated about a year after Percy

and I were married. It sounded like whoever wrote it had been corresponding with Aunt Mildred for some time."

"Can you remember any of it?"

Carol squinted and looked past me out the window. "The first part thanked Aunt Mildred for all her support and talked about how wonderful she was and what a great friend she'd been. Real sappy sweet." Carol met my gaze. "Don't get me wrong. Aunt Mildred was all those things, but I would've never been that gushy about it."

"Of course not," I said.

"Then it mentioned needing money. That the person's husband had been out of work. I think the amount was two hundred dollars."

"Did you ever ask your Aunt Mildred for money?"

"No, never. That's why it's so strange. The letter made it sound like it wasn't unusual. I wanted to crawl under a rock once I read it. I'd never send a letter to one of my relations asking for money. I'm no beggar." Carol raised her chin. "I was mortified when I saw that. What must have Aunt Mildred thought of me?" She fought back tears.

"I'm sure she loved you. Uncle Cyrus said she'd been fond of you and enjoyed being a part of your wedding. That she talked about it for months after."

Carol gave a slight smile. "That's kind of you to say, but it doesn't change the fact someone impersonating me asked her for money." Carol popped up out of the chair. "What if she wasn't the only one?" The color drained from her face.

"I'm sure it was an isolated incident," I consoled her.

She took a deep breath and let it out. "You think so?"

"Yes, I do." I waited for her to sit back down. "Now, what did the other letters say?"

"They read about the same. They'd thank her, give her a compliment or two, and then offer an explanation as to why the writer needed money. Then they'd name an amount." The towel on her head dangled a little further toward her shoulder. Carol pushed the towel back to the center of her head. "From the number of letters, it looked like it'd been going on for years." The tears reappeared. "For years. Can you imagine someone taking advantage of your aunt using your name and you not knowing it?" She swiped the tears from her cheeks and sniffled.

"Did you recognize the handwriting?" I asked because it had to be someone she knew well, since they knew about her relationship with her aunt.

"Well," she looked down at her hands in her lap. "It sort of looked … kind of …" then she shook her head. "No, never mind." She waved her hand in front of her to wave away the idea.

"No, go on. You never know what might help. And we do want to find Uncle Cyrus's attackers, so you can return home, right?"

"No, I know better. It couldn't be."

"It couldn't be who?" I pinned her with my gaze.

She squirmed in her seat. "I don't feel comfortable saying."

"Carol, you can trust me. I'm just looking for the truth."

She bit her lip. Carol wanted to tell me who she thought might be the author of those forged letters, but the door swung open and in stepped Percy and the oily teen before she had a chance.

Danny rolled his eyes when he spotted me. "What is she doing here?"

"Offering you a new place to stay. It's close to the town square, and I'm sure there will be plenty for you to do." The joyful gleam from earlier rushed back into her eyes.

"What? No, I don't want to go."

Relief flooded through me.

"I'm sorry, mister. But you're going. You've been complaining there's nothing for you to do here, and now you have an opportunity to explore the town. You're going."

"But—"

"No buts. Go pack a bag. I'll call you tomorrow to check in on you. Hopefully, it won't be long before they catch the person who did this to Uncle Cyrus, and we can go home. In the meantime, you're going to stay with Amy Kate and Cousin Julia."

The teen nailed me with a heated glare and turned to go to the bedroom at the end of the trailer.

"This is sure nice of you." Percy leaned against the counter that groaned under his weight. "You struck me as a kind person. Pretty as well as smart. It's nothing short of self-sacrificing of you to give the kid something to do."

For some reason, instead of feeling like a great person, I felt like a sucker being played. At least the kid was honest in his dislike of me. But Percy's flattery rubbed me the wrong way.

CHAPTER THIRTEEN

For the first few minutes, we meandered down the highway in silence. Danny gazed out the window at the pine trees and shrubs along the roadside. Then I felt his eyes studying me.

I glanced at him, wondering what he was thinking. It didn't take long for me to find out.

"What's a hot babe like you doing driving a beat-up, old Dodge Caravan? You don't have kids or something, do you?" Danny scowled and leaned back in the passenger seat. He crossed his right ankle over his left knee trying to look older than he was. "Because I don't go anywhere near crying babies." He held out his palms as a barrier.

"No worries. I don't have kids. Just a van." I thought it best to overlook the hot babe remark.

"Well then, that's all right." He wiggled his eyebrows at me.

I groaned and decided I liked him better as an obnoxious tattletale. Now, he reminded me of his dad. A shudder ran through me.

Danny inched closer to me, pulling against his seatbelt and placed his hand on top of mine on the steering wheel. "We could have some fun, you know." A cat-that-ate-the-canary grin wove its way across his lips.

A bolt of anger shot through me like a speeding bullet. How dare this little pipsqueak.

"Okay, let's." I jerked my steering wheel to the right, pulling my hand out from under his and whipped over into the emergency lane, then slammed on the brakes, sending Danny first forward and then backward in one fluid motion. Then I took off, swerving and weaving over the rumble strip that lined the edge of the emergency lane. For my finale, I crisscrossed over all three lanes of traffic, made a hard right, and threaded back again, screeching to a stop right before an on-ramp.

"Are you crazy? You could've killed me!" Danny screamed, the blood draining from his acne-scarred complexion.

"Don't tempt me." I turned in my seat, so he could see my face. With a low, steady tone, I meted out my words. "Here are the ground rules. First don't ever touch me. Second, don't call me babe, hot, hottie, sugar mama, or any other slang word for a woman you could possibly think of. You can call me Amy Kate or Ms. Anderson. Anything else, and you will be taking your life into your own hands. You are not to touch my things or Julia's, and if I find anything, I mean anything, missing I'm calling my boyfriend, the police detective. Have I made myself clear?"

The part about Gabe being my boyfriend I threw in for added glitter, but who knew? Maybe one day, we'd move beyond the getting-to-know-each-other stage.

Danny crossed his arms and slumped back against his seat. "Yeah, I got it."

I pulled the car back onto the highway in a subdued manner and looked for the off-ramp that led to the town square. Our apartment complex, Heartland Arms, was located a few blocks from Twisted Plots and the town green on the corner of Monroe Street and Lincoln Avenue.

Julia had left my dad's house before me around four.

She said she needed to catch up on some paperwork for her cake business, Pure Sweetness, and then planned to binge-watch a few episodes of the *Cold Case True Crime* show to relax.

Boy, was she in for a surprise. I glanced over at the brooding teen, hoping his hormones would level out before we reached the apartment. As I watched him out of the corner of my eye, it dawned on me this was the perfect opportunity to see what he knew about the holes in Uncle Cyrus's orchard. Well, that is, if he'd do more than grunt at me now that I'd scared him to death. "So, have you enjoyed your stay in Pine Lake?" I dipped my toe into the conversational pool as it were.

He glared at me from beneath a tight-knit brow and turned his attention back out the passenger window.

Clearing my throat, I tried again. "The weather has been great for the family reunion, don't you think?" I smiled.

"Are you for real? You're like a bad faucet." He huffed and shook his head. "Hot one minute and cold the next." He fished his phone out of his front pocket and opened it to a game.

My chances of finding out what he knew slipped away with each ping and zing. "Hey Danny, what did you think of Uncle Cyrus's visit Friday? Got any idea what those letters were about?"

He glanced up from the screen for a moment and then turned his shoulder toward me.

Rats. No dice.

"Come on. I'd like to know what you think," I said.

"Really? Okay then, I think you're a terrible driver, an eavesdropper, and a lunatic." He threw his hands above his head, not losing his grip on his phone.

I kept my cool. "Okay, that's fair, but you were acting like a jerk."

For some reason, this seemed to thaw him. He

shrugged. "Yeah, maybe. But my brother David says by the time he was my age, he'd already had three girlfriends and could go out with anyone at his high school that he wanted. He thinks I'm a loser."

"You're not a loser, and the fact he had girlfriends doesn't mean he knows beans about women. Besides, I'm not in high school."

"Yeah, I know. But I thought you might be an easy target to practice on. You know being older and alone. Thought you might be desperate. My older brother says when women reach a certain age, they get desperate."

"You think I'm a certain age?" The muscles in my jaw tensed.

He nodded. "With the wrinkles around your eyes." He pointed in their direction without touching them. "and, you know." He waved his hand in a circular motion near my face.

Forgetting all about the letters and Uncle Cyrus, I asked, "What? What else do you think makes me a woman of a certain age?" I frowned.

"You might want to watch all that frowning. It's bad for your face. Makes you age faster." He leaned back in his seat. "Besides, I didn't know you had a boyfriend."

I pulled into one of the parking spaces assigned to me and Julia, and Danny jumped out, grabbing his duffle bag from off the van floor.

He looked over at me. "Are you coming?"

"I'll be there in a minute. It's the door with the welcome mat with a picture of a pair of flip flops on it. 8A."

He nodded and shut the door.

Once Danny moved further down the breezeway, I pulled down the visor and opened the lighted mirror. The faint lines around my eyes stood out. Turning my head from side to side, I fingered the lines by my eyes and the ones by my mouth. Thirty loomed too close for comfort. I slammed the mirror shut and threw the visor back into place.

Rotten kid. Now, I'd never look at myself the same. Although I wasn't a spring chicken, I had no delusions, but I'd never ever thought of myself as a woman of a certain age. That described Aunt Maude or Julia's Great-aunt Emma. Not me.

I climbed from the van, hunched a little, and shuffled forward. One minute a hot babe, the next, Grandma Moses.

It was going to take a special knack to herd this teenager. I hoped Julia was up to the task.

CHAPTER FOURTEEN

The alarm rang, interrupting my dream about a ten-foot chicken chasing me as its feathers molted off its body into little gray clouds that rained droplets of anti-aging cream.

I groaned as I swung my feet out from under the covers and grabbed my robe to head to the bathroom. Imagine my surprise when I found it occupied.

The kid.

I pushed my arms through the sleeves of my robe, pulled the belt tight, and headed down the hall, Gizmo at my heels. Hanging a left in the living room into the kitchen, I went straight for the pot of coffee waiting for me on the counter and poured a steamy mug.

Julia, the saint, made coffee every day before she left for work in the wee hours of the morning.

I leaned over and scooped up Gizmo, who wagged his whole body with his usual morning enthusiasm.

The chicken dream haunted me. I half expected to find black and white feathers littering the floor and smudges of anti-aging cream all over the appliances.

Before I took more than a few sips of my coffee, the bathroom door creaked open. I scurried down the hall with

Gizmo in my arms, passing the oily teen on my way. He didn't even acknowledge my existence as I brushed past him nearly spilling the contents of my mug. With his eyes closed and his arms extended, he somehow missed the coffee table and made it back to the couch.

Gizmo squirmed, so I put him down. The instant his paws hit the floor; he ran down the hall toward the couch but didn't jump on it. Instead, he stopped and sniffed the boy's feet.

When I finished my morning routine, I peeked down the hall from the bathroom doorway and found Danny sprawled out on the couch, looking more like a murder victim and less like someone's sleeping child. The urge to check his pulse washed over me, but when he moaned and rolled to his side, I headed back to my room to finish getting ready for work.

Having a teen in the house would take some getting used to. Hopefully, it wouldn't be for long. Julia had taken the news about our guest rather well, considering the circumstances.

When I emerged, dressed and half caffeinated, Danny was sitting in an upright position with his eyes closed and his head laid back on the couch cushion. Gizmo sat next to him. "Danny?" I moved toward him. "Are you awake?"

"No."

"Well, I need to leave in a few minutes. Do you want some breakfast? You know it's the most important meal of the day." A feeling of déjà vu rushed over me. How many times did my mother said those very words to me when I was Danny's age?

"No."

"Did you see Julia before she left for the bed and breakfast?"

"No."

I went into the kitchen and dug around in the junk drawer until I found the spare key. Actually, it's the spare,

spare key. We kept one under the flip-flop welcome mat, but I didn't want Danny to know that. I'd rather give him a key he's responsible for in case things go missing. Like Grandma's fine china or money from glass jars.

Gizmo jumped off the couch and came to me when I entered the living room. "Here, I found a key for you to use. If you leave, lock the door, and don't let Gizmo out. He likes to sneak over to visit the cute little poodle around the corner."

"Umm."

So much for pulling any information out of him in this condition.

"I can get you a cup of coffee if it might help." I stood behind one of the overstuffed chairs, watching him. Finally, one eye slid open.

"I don't want any coffee, or breakfast, or a dog licking my toes." He growled, "I want to go back to sleep. Julia woke me up at five thirty with all her noise. Humming and banging around in the kitchen."

Gizmo barked.

I grinned. Ah, yes. Julia and her morning rays of happiness. "Guess I should've warned you Julia tends to be a morning person."

He cut slitted eyes at me and placed a throw pillow over his face.

"Look, I'm sorry about Julia, but there's something I wanted to talk to you about."

He dropped his arm letting the pillow fall back to the couch. "If I answer, will you quit torturing me and let me go back to sleep?"

"Yes." I stepped around the chair and took a seat. "I wanted to know what your mom said about those letters Uncle Cyrus showed her. Did she talk about them after we left?"

He raised his head. "My dad was curious about them, so yeah, she talked about them with him."

I sat waiting. "Well, what did she say?"

"Really, you want me to rat out my own parents?"

Okay, the kid had a point. "Look, I'm simply looking for the truth. From what I heard—"

"Eavesdropping," Danny interjected.

I ignored his attempt to make me feel guilty. "It sounded like your mom didn't write the other letters."

"Maybe she did but didn't want Uncle Cyrus to know. Did you think about that?" He paused to throw me a scowl, then continued. "She told Dad all the letters were asking for money. I guess she said she hadn't written them because she didn't want anyone to know she'd been asking our relatives for help." Danny slid back down onto the couch and stretched out. "Dad wasn't happy about it."

"What do you mean?" I pressed.

"He got real uptight. Told her not to talk to Cyrus again about them. He didn't want people thinking he couldn't provide for his family."

I leaned back in the chair not sure how to interrupt this information.

"Can I go back to sleep now?"

"Have you seen the letters since then?" I asked.

He turned his head my direction. "What do you mean? Are the letters missing?"

"Maybe." I shrugged and took an interest in my nails.

"Look, I don't even have my driver's license. How am I supposed to have gotten out to Uncle Cyrus's house to steal the letters?"

"I thought you were old enough to drive," I said in my defense.

"No, my stepbrother, David, is the one you're thinking of. He's in his thirties. Mom says I was her bonus baby." He rolled onto his back.

Surprised by the large age difference, I asked, "How old are you?"

"I'm sixteen."

"Going on twenty-five," I added.

A smile spread across his lips and traveled up to his eyes. The first smile I'd seen on his face, and it looked good on him.

"You should smile more. Makes you less scary. More friendly. Maybe it'd help you with the girls."

"Maybe, but it'd freak my mom out." He chuckled and grabbed the wadded-up blanket off the floor and spread it over his legs.

I looked at my watch and stood. Late, again. Flora would be ready with a lecture on punctuality. She prided herself on her reliability, and I depended on it. "I'd better go." I walked to the coat rack in the corner behind the front door and pulled my purse from one of its arms. But before I opened the door, a thought struck me. "Danny, the other day when you found me outside the R.V., you asked me something that I didn't understand."

"Hm?" His eyes were closed again.

"You asked me if I were one of your dad's friends. What did you mean by that? Who are your dad's friends, and why would they be looking for him here? At the reunion?"

"I don't know. Guess I was confused." Danny rolled over onto his side, and Gizmo jumped up onto the other end of the couch. Turning three times, he settled on top of the super-sized feet of the teen.

Opening the door, I walked through the breezeway to the Mom-mobile. The answers Danny gave me didn't fit into the puzzle as I'd hoped. They left me more unsure. Did Carol lie to Cyrus to cover up the fact she had asked Mildred for financial help?

My gut said Percy had something to do with the attack on Cyrus, but why would a middle-aged man go on a digging expedition in broad daylight?

Of course, my gut had thought Danny was involved with the assault, but now I couldn't see it. Guess there were more ways of getting red clay dirt under one's fingernails than digging up pickle jars full of money.

CHAPTER FIFTEEN

When I entered Twisted Plots, two customers waited at the counter to be checked out, and Flora was in the thriller section helping an older gentleman. The looks on the faces of the two at the register told me they'd been waiting longer than a minute. "I'll be right with you." I rushed through to the workroom to deposit my purse on my desk.

A yellow sticky note that sat in the middle of my desk calendar caught my eye. It read: *Chet Baker called. Will stop by before noon.*

Interesting. Chet Baker and I had a bumpy but humorous relationship. He had been one of my online matches with the Open Hearts dating service. But when we went out, he turned out to be a reporter for the *Pine Lake Daily* newspaper, trying to get a scoop about the fire and murder. Let's just say we both ended up with mud on our faces that day.

I smiled. With his blond hair and *GQ* style, even mud couldn't hide his good looks. If it hadn't been for a certain detective and the fact I wasn't sure I could trust Chet, I would've gone out on a second date with him. I put the sticky note back on the desk and went to rescue Flora and the waiting customers.

By eleven, the foot traffic slowed, but a few browsers were taking their time looking at the cards and specialty gift items.

Flora had skipped the lecture on punctuality and instead quizzed me about the teen, Danny. "So, you don't think he's your second attacker?" Flora rolled her mouse around and clicked on the screen, searching for a first edition for Mrs. Darcy, our resident collector.

"No, I can't see it. He's surly and hormonal, but that describes all teenagers."

Flora chuckled. "Yeah, pretty much. At least my boys went through a stage like that. Thank goodness they're grown with their own lives now."

"Yes, but you have those two grandbabies coming up." I grabbed another stack of the latest thriller book and walked over to the display table. Spreading the books out over the surface, I laid the groundwork for the book pyramid I needed to build.

The bell on the door clanged, and I glanced up to find Chet Baker walking into the bookshop. He wore a blue polo shirt, khaki pants, and loafers. His blond hair contained enough product to keep the salons in business for years. Not a hair out of place. He carried in his hand a manila file folder.

"Hey there. How's my favorite date?"

I rolled my eyes. "Doing pretty good. Did you ever remove all the mud from your pants?"

His lips widened into a smile and displayed a row of straight, white teeth. "Why yes, I did. But it did cost me a pretty penny at the dry cleaners." He met my gaze. "Did you ever find out about that rogue raccoon?"

"No, I didn't." I turned and headed back to the counter to retrieve another stack of books. "How can I help you?" I asked over my shoulder.

Chet followed me and grabbed a stack as well. "I heard

through the grapevine you were out at Cyrus Jacobs' when he was attacked. Is that true?"

I stopped. "You heard that through the grapevine?"

"Yeah, it's been working overtime since the skeleton was found. You should hear what they're saying about poor Gary Martin."

I plopped the books onto the table. "What are they saying?"

Flora ambled over from the science fiction section. "Yeah, what are they saying?"

"What, you don't know?" I looked at her, confused. "You always know what's going on in this town."

Flora crossed her arms. "Usually, but I want to make sure what he's heard is right. You can't depend on everyone getting the facts straight. You know how people love to glom onto a subject and add their own opinions as gospel truth."

Chet smiled. "I appreciate that, Flora."

"So, what did you hear?" Flora asked.

"I heard the day Mildred disappeared, she'd been scheduled to go on a trip. Some kind of Bible convention or lady's retreat. Anyway, several sources—"

"Is that what we're calling them now, sources?" I grinned and raised my eyebrows.

The lopsided smile he gave me caused my heart to rev up a notch. Just slightly and only for a moment. Not like when Gabe gives me a boyish grin, but more like an uncontrollable response to something pleasant. At least, that's my story.

"Yes. They said that at the time of Mildred's disappearance, a rumor ran around town that Gary Martin was having an affair. Everyone assumed the other woman was Mildred. If it were true, it would give the DA a motive for Cyrus killing her."

I frowned and picked up two books, placing them one on top of the other at an angle. "From what Cyrus has said, it sounds like the marriage was solid."

"Can you believe him? I mean if he's the killer."

"You weren't there when he realized the body was Mildred. He couldn't fake that unless he was an award-winning actor. No, his shock was genuine."

"Okay. So, if Cyrus didn't kill her, who did?" Chet asked.

"Well, that's what Amy Kate's trying to figure out," Flora answered in my defense.

Chet set the books down and handed me the manila folder. "I found these clippings from when Mildred first disappeared. I figured Julia would have you looking into it. Maybe these can help you."

A funny feeling niggled in my gut as I took the folder from him. "What do you get out of it?"

"Who, me?" Chet put his hands to his chest and feigned being insulted.

"Yes, you. What do you want in return for these articles? Remember, I know you. We've dated." I placed my fist on my hip and cocked my head to the side, giving him the stink eye.

His expression softened. "First interview with the killer."

"That would be up to the police." I held his gaze.

"All right. How about an exclusive with Cyrus once he's feeling up to it?"

"Umm, that may be harder than getting the interview with the killer. You know how stubborn the man can be."

"Muleheaded," Flora said.

"But I'll see what I can do. Of course, that's assuming …" I let my words drift away because I didn't want to state the possible outcome. I didn't want to think we might lose Cyrus. It hung in the air, anyway.

Julia sent me an update on him before I arrived at work. He was doing as well as could be expected. Still in the coma, but the doctors held out great hope for a recovery. I wanted to hold out great hope, too.

With Chet's help, I finished up with the book pyramid, and we took the file folder to the back workroom so we could spread out the contents onto the wooden worktable.

Chet slid onto the stool, and I sat across from him on the other one. I flipped open the folder and pulled out several articles from the *Pine Lake Daily*. There were also a few from other papers from nearby towns. Apparently, Cyrus had run some missing persons ads in them.

"See?" I pushed the missing persons ads toward Chet. "If he killed her, why would he draw any unneeded attention to the case?"

"Maybe he was covering his tracks. Wanted it to look like she'd left and used this as a way to plant that idea in other people's minds."

"Remind me never to make you mad. You could figure out too clever a plan to dispose of a body."

"Thank you?" Chet said.

I perused the other articles. One was about Mildred's disappearance and the reward Cyrus offered for information. A picture of Cyrus and Mildred out in the orchard accompanied the article. Cyrus wore a jacket.

"Wait here." I slipped out of my seat and called down the hall to Flora. "Can you come here for a minute? I want you to see something."

Flora appeared a few minutes later. "What do you need?"

"Do you remember what you told me the other day about Cyrus's jacket?" I glanced toward Chet to signal her to be cryptic. Flora caught on quick.

"Oh, the jacket. Yes."

"Is this the one?" I handed her the article with the picture.

"Yes, but it looks much shorter. It seemed longer when I noticed it." She stretched the word out to three syllables.

"Um, interesting." I said.

Chet leaned back in the stool and crossed his arms. "I take it there is something you'd rather I didn't know. Well, there's the thanks I get for helping."

"Now, Chet, you do get an exclusive. When I can, I'll explain more."

Flora shot me a pleading look, and I added, "If I can."

Chet leaned forward and placed his elbows on the table. "Fine. I'm patient. I can wait. But I want to know the minute I can talk with Cyrus. This murder and assault have been the biggest news in town since your last tangle with a dead body. Seems murder tends to find you, Amy Kate."

Flora laughed. "Son, you don't know the half of it. This girl attracts trouble like honey attracts flies. Has since she was in high school. Do you know she sent one of her prom dates to the emergency room?"

"I can believe that." Chet raised his eyebrows and nodded. "I've had my own close encounter." His eyes met mine. "But after the initial shock, it wasn't so bad."

My cheeks flamed under the intensity of his scrutiny, so much so that I feared the heat radiating from me might set the old articles in my hand ablaze. So, when I heard the bell on the front door jingle, I jumped off my stool glad for an excuse to make my escape.

But when Gabe's voice floated down the hall, the awkwardness of the moment amplified by ten, and I cringed, not sure what to do.

CHAPTER SIXTEEN

Gabe entered the back workroom, his brown curls tangled, and his suit coat thrown over his shoulder.

"Oh, I didn't know you were having a party back here." He surveyed the small group and nodded. "Chet."

"Gabe." Chet pushed his stool back. Then glancing from Gabe to me, he stood. "Guess I'd better get going. I wanted to deliver the articles. Thought they might be of some help."

"Yes, thanks." With one move, I gathered the clippings and copies spread across the table and tucked them back into the file folder.

"I'd better get back out front before someone runs off with the whole store." Flora shot me a look, then scurried down the hall to the front.

"If I didn't know better, I'd think you were up to something." Gabe moved toward me, throwing his suitcoat over the back of the other stool. "But you're not, right?" He pinned me with his stare before taking me by my shoulders and touching my cheek with his thumb.

"Well, I do have some new information. But to be clear, I was going to share it with you. Like we agreed."

Gabe's face lit up, and he pulled me into his arms.

"Good. I knew I could count on you to cooperate."

His arms felt so good around me. It would be so easy to get used to this. To hope for a future full of warm hugs and protective declarations. But so far, we hadn't talked about a tomorrow together. We were too busy trying to connect today. Our date Saturday night popped into my brain.

As if he'd read my mind, he asked, "Are we still on for Saturday?"

I stepped back. "That's part of the new information I have for you."

A frown settled on his face as his eyebrows merged. "Okay?" He sat on the stool behind him. "What's up?"

"Well, Julia's cousin, Danny, is staying with us. Just until you give them the green light they can go home. So, I'm not sure if I'll be able to go Saturday night with all of Julia's family still in town. I should help her keep them entertained or something." I paused to see how Gabe was digesting this information.

"How did this happen?" Gabe shot up. "Why is Danny White staying at your apartment? He's a potential suspect in the assault."

"Well ..." I stammered.

Gabe crossed his arms and widened his stance. "You've put yourself and Julia in a dangerous situation. You can't trust that kid."

"He seems harmless."

"Well, Mr. Harmless has a record as long as my arm for petty thief and carjacking."

"Danny told me this morning he couldn't drive. He doesn't have a license," I said.

"He doesn't. It's suspended. At least he was honest about that." Gabe lifted his eyebrows, and the frown on his lips smoothed out into a straight line of resignation. "So, how did he end up at your house?"

I stared down at my high heels wanting to be anywhere

else but here. "I sort of invited him."

Gabe shook his head.

"I needed an excuse to talk to Carol about the letters. Otherwise she'd have known I was looking into Cyrus's attack. She still says she didn't write them. At least the ones Cyrus had."

Gabe plopped back onto the stool, still shaking his head. "What else did you find out?"

"That the other letters contained requests for money from Mildred." I stood next to Gabe and leaned my elbow on the table. "Carol denied writing them, but I wonder if she lied so Percy wouldn't know she'd been asking her family for money."

"That's a good point."

There was no way I was telling him Mr. Harmless had been the one to suggest this possibility. I continued, "I had to come up with an excuse other than the letters for me being there, so I offered to let Danny stay with us since the R.V. is pretty small. I never dreamed they'd accept."

"Well, they did. So, be careful, and whatever you do, don't leave him in the house alone. And don't give him a key. It'd be like giving Dracula free rein in a blood bank."

My stomach dropped to my feet, my mind whirling through the valuable items in the apartment. There weren't many, but my grandmother's china and her silver spoons did top the list.

Gabe studied me. "What's wrong?"

"Nothing. I've got it covered." I moved to my overstuffed chair in the corner of the room. "Was there a reason you stopped by?" I asked, wanting to end the conversation so I could dash home to hide the silver.

"Yeah, I've been thinking about those letters, too. And there's something I can't figure out."

"What is it?" I asked.

"Why did Carol write the letters?"

"I just told you, because she was asking for money." I

scowled. Gabe wasn't usually this thick.

"No, why write? Why not call?" Gabe walked towards the second overstuffed chair and sat across from me. "If you're asking for money, why write? Wouldn't you want to call, so you could plead your case in person, so to speak?"

"Oh." I sat up. "I see your point. If I wanted to convince someone to do something, I'd want to talk to them, not write a letter and wait and see if they'd do it. Especially if I were asking for money."

"Right. Because when someone asks for money, they tend to need it right away." Gabe leaned his forearms on his knees. "So, what's up with the pen pal approach?"

I slumped back in my chair, puzzled by the question. Why the letters? Why not the phone?

Gabe answered his own question. "The way I figure it, Carol is telling us the truth. She didn't write the letters. And the reason to write instead of phone is to hide your identity."

"That makes sense. Okay, Sherlock. If it wasn't Carol, then who?" I asked.

"Do you remember anything about the envelope? Like the postmark on the stamp. Where it came from?"

Oh, so this was the reason for his visit. I'd seen one of the letters. "Remember, the only one I saw Carol says she wrote."

"Yeah, but where did it come from?"

I closed my eyes and tried to recall the front of the envelope. Why hadn't I snapped a picture of it when I had it? I won't make that mistake again.

"I think it was St. Louis, but I can't be sure." I opened my eyes and met Gabe's gaze.

"Yeah, that's what I thought. St. Louis. If that's where Carol lived, then the person sending the letters would have mailed them from St. Louis which means—"

"That the letter impersonator has to be one of her own family."

"Correct." Gabe leaned back in his chair and gave me a winner-takes-all smile. "So, it's either Percy or Carol. Danny wouldn't have been born yet."

"Wait. There's an older stepbrother, David. He's in his thirties."

"No, the math doesn't work. He would've been a small child around the time in question." Gabe rubbed the back of his neck. "No, it's either Carol or Percy who sent those letters, and my guess is Percy."

"Well, how does that help us with Mildred's case?"

"Motive. Whoever was asking for money from her on a regular basis could've decided they needed more. Or maybe she refused to keep sending the money. Either way, it gives the letter writer motive for killing her."

Interesting, Danny, the oily teen, has a record, and perhaps one of his parents is a murderer. Julia wasn't going to like this new development in her family tree. A family twist of huge proportions.

Gabe stood. "I'll ask Floyd to look into Percy White's past a little deeper. There has to be something we're missing."

"Good and I might go talk to Julia's Great-aunt Emma. She'd know where Carol and Percy were living during that time, and whether or not Percy had steady employment."

"That's a good idea." Gabe moved toward the doorway, then stopped, his jaw set. "And I'm keeping our plans for Saturday night. I don't care how many Jacobs are in town." He pivoted and disappeared down the hall.

Great, just great. I plopped back onto the soft chair. Now, I'd have to figure out some other way to call off the date because I couldn't leave Julia in a lurch. If we didn't solve the murder by Saturday, her relatives would turn into a howling mob, wanting to return to their real lives. She'd need my help.

I heaved a sigh and scooted up from the chair. In light of Gabe's ultimatum, my only option was to find the killer.

Simple as that.

CHAPTER SEVENTEEN

After Gabe left, I grabbed the file folder containing the articles from the worktable. Dad always taught us girls to use all our resources, and I counted Flora Smith-Jones as a valuable resource full of odds and ends about the people of Pine Lake.

Entering the main area of the bookshop, I found her in the romance section. "Flora, if you don't mind, would you look through these articles with me? I figured you'd know much more about the people than I would."

A sparkle appeared in her eyes. "I'd be glad to help. You know I love nothing better than a good puzzle." She hurried over to the counter and placed two copies of the latest romance near the computer. "Besides, my heart goes out to Cyrus. I can't fathom how he must feel. I mean, before the coma."

"Of course," I said.

I laid the photocopies of the old articles and the few originals from the file, across the dark wood. "Let's put them in chronological order."

Flora scooted the pieces of paper around until the dates were in ascending order. "Seems the first article came out the Tuesday after Cyrus reported her missing." She picked up the copy of an article that had been printed the Friday after Mildred's disappearance. "Look, it says here the police were calling it a missing persons case."

"Yeah, Dad told me yesterday they couldn't find any evidence pointing to a murder. No blood stains, no weapon, nothing that pointed to foul play."

"Gosh, that's after your dad had been promoted to detective. So young." Flora sighed. "Where has the time gone?" She peered back at the article in her hand. "Hm, says that Cyrus claimed when he left to go to Guntersville that morning, she had a suitcase packed and ready to go to the women's retreat."

"It makes sense. I mean, that she packed it. It explains why all the right items were gone."

Flora's face crumpled into a web of lines. "What do you mean?"

"Something Dad said. The police ruled out murder because all the right things were missing. Her hairbrush, her toothbrush, her favorite ring, and the suitcase itself. They were all items she herself would've packed."

"Still not seeing the big picture," Flora said.

"If someone like Cyrus had killed her and then tried to pack the suitcase to make it look like she'd run off, he'd have forgotten something. He'd have packed the wrong stuff. But since all the right stuff was gone, they figured she'd left town."

"Well, those crazy rumors about Mildred and Gary didn't help. And boy, did his wife kick up some dust over it. The jealous type. Once, she found him in Hooks Restaurant eating dinner with another woman. The yelling and name calling were legendary. She even went so far as to throw a drink in the other woman's face."

"Was he cheating on her?"

"I don't know, but later it came out the woman from the restaurant was a client. Gary's a lawyer. But since it was a dinner engagement, and they met at one of the most romantic places in Pine Lake—"

"I know. The ambiance is great." I sighed, wondering if Gabe had considered that spot for our date, the one I needed to cancel.

"Definitely. Trudy, his wife, read more into it. Not too long after that, he left for Texas."

"That's interesting." More pieces to toss in the puzzle box. "Do you remember when that was? When they moved?"

Flora squinted and puckered her lips. "Not too long before Mildred went missing. That's why the rumors were flying about those two. She went missing right after Gary up and closed his practice and left for Texas. Trudy stayed behind. I think to sell the house."

"That must've been tough for Cyrus. To hear all those rumors while he was torn apart with worry."

"Well, that's part of the reason why I didn't tell anyone what I saw that day when I passed by Cyrus's house. He kept insisting something happened to her. The man wouldn't let it go. So, if he'd been the one to kill her, he'd never carry on the way he did."

"True. Why would a murderer who was about to get away with it keep insisting there was a murder?"

"Exactly. I figured Cyrus had simply gotten his return time from Guntersville wrong and the person I saw was him, working on the property. But with the stand of trees that used to be there obscuring the view, I can't be sure who I saw."

The picture of Cyrus and Mildred lay to my left. I picked it up and pointed to Cyrus. "So, the orange jacket. You said it was longer on the person you saw that day."

"Yeah, here it hits Cyrus at the hips where it's supposed to, but that day, I could've sworn it went closer to his knees. It looked too big for him. Of course, like I said, I was driving and maybe going a hair over the speed limit, so I only caught a split-second glimpse."

"There had to be something about what you saw that struck you or you wouldn't have remembered it for so long." I studied my gray-haired friend. "I want you to think back. Did anything else stand out?"

Flora leaned her elbows on the counter and closed her eyes. If I hadn't known better, I'd swear she was praying, and maybe she was. "The shovel. There was a shovel."

"Great, that's good. I think you can prove Cyrus is innocent. It wasn't him you saw. It was our killer. And if Cyrus's coat hung to their thighs, then they're much shorter." I studied the picture I held. "Yeah, a lot shorter. Maybe our killer is a woman."

"But wasn't it a guy who ran through the hallway at Cyrus's the other day?"

"Yes, but Carol has several men in the family she could've sent to retrieve the letters for her. Or maybe the two events aren't connected," I said.

"No." Flora shook her head. "None of this started until the reunion."

"True. But the remains being found right before the reunion makes it seem as if they are connected. They could just as easily not be."

"Maybe," Flora said, "but my money is on the writer of those letters. Find the letters. Find the killer."

CHAPTER EIGHTEEN

I slipped by the apartment and checked on Mr. Harmless for myself to make sure he hadn't taken off with the china, our jewelry, or worse, Gizmo. To my relief, Grandma's things were still where I had left them. Danny, however, was not.

The note he'd left on the table told me he'd gone to find some lunch. I took Gizmo out, then left.

Arriving at the south end of town at a gated, assisted-living community called The Golden Hills, I pushed the button on the intercom outside of the black metal gate. A voice boomed over the squeaky rumble emitting from the small gray box. "Can I help you?"

"Yes, I'm here to—"

The voice cut in. "I'm sorry, dear. I can't hear you. You'll have to speak up."

I rolled my window further down, so I could lean the upper portion of my body out of the van. Bracing myself inches away from the box, I tried again. "I'm here to see Emma Jacobs ..." I paused. Great-aunt Emma's married name escaped me. "Well, she was Emma Jacobs, but I can't remember her married name."

"Hm, sounds suspicious to me," the voice accused.

"I know her as Aunt Emma," I said.

"Well, if she's your aunt, you should know her last name."

"Actually, she's not my aunt."

"Then why are you here? You can't go around claiming people willy-nilly as your aunt. Is this some kind of prank? 'cause I got a garden hose, and I'm not afraid to use it, kiddo." The squeaking noise from the other end ceased.

I pushed the button again. No answer. I pushed again and waited. No answer. Determined to talk to Aunt Emma, I tried one last time.

A moment later, the voice barked, "Go away."

"Look, call her and tell her Amy Kate Anderson is here to see her. If she says no, I'll leave."

The squeaking persisted. "Fine. I'll call, but young lady, you really should know the names of your relatives."

The box went silent, and I lowered myself back into the van. My stomach grumbled in protest since I hadn't taken the time to eat lunch.

The voice came back and announced, "She'll see you." The woman also gave me Emma's address. Which helped since I didn't know that either.

The gate opened, and I proceeded through at the recommended speed of a snail. The community consisted of rows and rows of condominium-type homes where they share a wall, but they were much smaller and all one level.

I looked for the street, Meadow Park Lane, as I cruised down the main brick thoroughfare. A quick turn left and I spotted the black numbers for the address on the crisp white mailbox. Pulling up beside it, I parked.

Aunt Emma could be difficult at the best of times, so showing up without an invitation did not work in my favor. Add in the call from the gatekeeper, and I wasn't sure what kind of welcome I'd receive. I grabbed my purse and sent up a little prayer on my jaunt up the driveway.

The teal-colored front door swung open before I had the chance to knock. "Well, Amy Kate, to what do I owe this pleasure? Let me guess. You're here trying to find out who put Cyrus in the hospital."

"Yes, ma'am. That's part of it."

"Well, I hope you don't think it was me. These days, I can barely lift my frying pans. Don't think I could knock anyone on the head hard enough to hurt, much less put them in a coma."

"Have you heard news about Cyrus?" I asked, hoping she might have a more up-to-date report.

"No," Aunt Emma stepped out of the way to let me enter. "I haven't heard anything today. But Thomas has been keeping me informed. You might as well come in. I was sitting down to lunch if you'd like a grilled cheese sandwich."

"Sounds good."

The foyer of the little house held a coat rack, a small table with a mirror hanging above it, and an old family picture that hung on the wall. Emma led the way to the kitchen, but I stopped to look at the photograph. "Who are these people?"

Emma backtracked to the foyer. "Oh, these are my children. This one here is me, and that's my husband, Matthew. The tallest boy is Leo, then this is Earl, and that's Carol. She was maybe six in that picture. Had the prettiest blonde hair." She turned and went back to the kitchen.

I followed and pulled out a chair at the small round table. The bright green tablecloth covering it highlighted the cheery yellow walls.

Emma pulled out the cheese and butter from the refrigerator and grabbed the bread out of a basket at the end of the counter. The skillet sizzled when she added the butter.

"So, I was wondering about something you said the other day at the reunion." I decided the direct approach would be best with Aunt Emma."

"You'll have to be more specific. I said a lot of things over the last few days at the reunion." She glanced my way and smiled.

For eighty-two, the woman was sharp. "It was about Carol and Percy. You said Percy used to have a bad habit. Can you tell me what kind of habit? I mean, did he used to smoke but gave it up?"

Emma squished the sandwich in the skillet with her spatula. "Did I say that?"

"Yes, you did. You said he had a bad habit."

Emma tensed. "Well, I meant he used to." She shrugged and flipped the sandwich.

"You mean he used to but doesn't now?" I asked.

She bobbed her head.

"If you don't mind me asking, what kind of bad habit did he have?"

She turned away from me and faced the stove. "He would sometimes—not very often, you understand—but occasionally play the lotto cards."

"Oh, that doesn't sound that bad." I hung my purse on the back of the chair and leaned my elbows on the tablecloth.

"Um, it did cause some tension between him and Carol, though. Especially, when he'd go across state lines to buy them."

"He had to cross state lines? I thought most states have a lottery."

"Not in the eighties. All this happened right after they got married. He'd drive over to Illinois and make a weekend of it. That's what caused the issues." Emma placed the sandwich on a plate and set it in front of me.

So, they lived in Missouri even then.

"Thank you. This looks good." My stomach grumbled its agreement.

"Eat up. You don't want it to get cold." She returned to

the stove and buttered two pieces of bread to make one for herself. "But like I said—" She grinned at me. "Once Carol made it clear she didn't want him gambling, he stopped. I think he realized he was married and needed to be more responsible with his money for his son's and new wife's sake."

I took a bite of the sandwich and swallowed. The melted cheese tasted delicious. "Was he able to quit? I mean, it sounds like he was kind of a serious gambler if he'd drive over the state lines to participate in the lottery. And what did he do the whole weekend?"

Emma joined me at the table. "I don't know, dear. I didn't ask Carol. She's defensive about their marriage since I didn't go to the wedding." A sadness passed over her eyes. "I've always regretted that decision. I thought maybe if I threatened not to come, she'd reconsider. But instead she went ahead without me."

"So, you didn't want her to marry Percy?" I asked between bites.

"No, I thought she could've done better. They've always had to scrape by. But I should've gone anyway. She's my only daughter, and our relationship has never been the same." Her voice shook, and she cleared her throat to hide it.

"What can you tell me about Carol's and Mildred's relationship? Were they close?"

Emma rose from her chair. "Where are my manners? Do you want something to drink? I have iced tea, water, and there's a cola in here that Earl left behind the other day."

"Water will be fine." I noticed she hadn't answered my question. So, I tried again. "Were Mildred and Carol close?"

Closing the refrigerator door with her foot, Emma walked over to the table and set down two glasses of water. "Yes, in a way. Perhaps it was because they were both in a relationship with older men. They seemed to gravitate to each other. Mildred understood her."

"How much older is Percy than Carol?"

"Oh, about eight years. Not like Cyrus and Mildred. She was somewhere near twenty-six or twenty-seven and Cyrus was thirty-nine. He took a lot of guff marrying someone so much younger." Emma tsked. "Everyone thought she was after his money. Figured she'd divorce him within a few years. But he proved us all wrong. They were married ten years before she disappeared."

This information confirmed what Flora and others had told me about Cyrus and Mildred. "Why do you think Carol would've written Mildred all those letters asking for money?"

A sour expression crossed Emma's face. "She wouldn't have. Carol is hardworking and proud. Too proud to ever beg for money. And that's what I told Cyrus at the reunion when he asked the same question."

"So, you don't think those letters to Mildred were written by Carol?"

"No, I do not." Emma raised her chin and folded her hands in front of her plate.

"Well, someone wrote them." I chewed the last bite of my sandwich, pondering who could've written the letters. "So, Percy used to gamble but quit once Carol threatened to leave him."

"Yes, but that was years ago." Emma took a sip from her glass.

"True, but so was Mildred's murder."

She set the glass down with a thud. "I don't like your tone, Amy Kate. What are you driving at?" She scowled.

"Are you sure he quit? If someone is addicted, it takes a lot more than simple self-discipline to stop. I knew a guy once in college whom everyone thought was a straight arrow, but then he got caught one evening with a pocketful of drugs. He swore it was his first time. But after the cops did some digging, it turned out he was the ringleader."

"What are you saying? That my son-in-law is some kind of criminal mastermind? Please." Emma rolled her eyes. "Have you ever spent any time with the man?"

I shook off the creepy tingles that ran over me at the thought of spending even one minute with the guy.

"All I'm saying is people aren't what you think. If you dig deep enough, you find more layers, and some of them hold some pretty dark secrets."

"Let me tell you what'cha'd find if you dug into Percy White's layers. A big chunk of nothing. He barely has one layer, much less two or three. No, if he said he quit, he quit. Besides, it's been close to forty years. There's no way he could hide something like that from Carol for so long."

I hated to admit it, but she had a point. It would've been hard to hide something like gambling for decades. Not impossible, but hard. On the other hand, when Mildred disappeared, it had only been a few years. He could've still been gambling then, even if he didn't now. Once I left Emma Jacobs Ross's house, I called the handsome Gabe the Babe, of the Pine Lake Police Department to give him the promised update. And, well, because I needed his help.

CHAPTER NINETEEN

Why use a shovel for digging out layers when you have a backhoe at your disposal? I pressed Gabe's number on my speed dial. He picked up after two rings. Nice.

"Hey, I was thinking about you," Gabe said.

"Good." The simple sound of his voice woke up the butterflies in my stomach. They fluttered around enough to stir up a few giggles.

"You sound happy," he said.

"I shouldn't. I just left Emma's house."

"What did you find out?" He shuffled some papers near the phone.

When the noise settled down, I answered, "Not much. She basically said the same thing Flora told me about Mildred and Carol and the wedding. But she did tell me Percy used to be a heavy gambler. Well, I say heavy. She didn't think it was that serious. But she did mention Carol was willing to leave him over it."

"Interesting."

A picture of his warm brown eyes full of adoration for my great detective work popped into my mind. "Plus, she mentioned he would make trips across the state line into Illinois to buy lottery tickets. Thing is, he'd make a weekend of it."

"Hm, sounds like he might have been buying them and taking them into his state to sell."

"You think?" Percy didn't strike me as the mastermind type—I agreed with Emma—but he did strike me as the sneaky type.

"Possibly. Hold on."

I could tell Gabe had covered his phone with his hand.

"Let me check around and see what I can find out about Percy and his alleged gambling habit."

"Do you think it has anything to do with Mildred or Cyrus?"

"Maybe. Look, I need to go. We got a call about some teens down by the lake."

"Sure. I'll talk to you later."

"Great. And be sure to circle Saturday night in red. I'm serious about keeping our date." The timber of his voice, low and strong, sent tingles dancing across my skin.

The instant I hung up; guilt washed over me. How could I leave Julia to deal with a mob of angry relatives and a teenage houseguest she hadn't asked for, on top of everything else, by herself. I couldn't.

I checked the dashboard. Two o'clock in the afternoon. If I hurried, I could still make the post office run to ship out our website orders. After joining Open Hearts dating services, it dawned on me what a great tool the internet could be for Twisted Plots. Sure, I wanted foot traffic, but in today's world, business is done online.

Kirk, my resident college employee, said he knew a guy, who knew a guy, who was a genius with Web design. Boy, was he right. The website captured my love for books and community in a way that I never could have.

The parking spot in front of Twisted Plots sat open, which I considered good and bad all at the same time.

Flora accosted me the instant I stepped over the threshold. "Amy Kate, I'm so glad you're here." She checked her watch. "I have something I want to tell you." She paused and glanced around to see who might overhear us. "We'd better step to the counter. It's about Mildred."

The three ladies in the romance section and the man in the home décor area didn't even look up.

She moved toward the counter where Carter stood, using the computer.

He looked up and smiled. "Hey, kiddo, heard you were out looking into what happened to Cyrus."

I stopped in front of the counter and placed my purse on it. "Yeah, I went to talk to Julia's Great-aunt Emma."

His eyes widened. "That should've been interesting. I hear she's a pistol."

"She is. But she grows on you." Emma had been kind to me and shared her lunch when she didn't have to, and anyone who shares food with me in my book can't be all bad.

"Guess who I saw earlier today coming out of the Beans and Leaves next door?" Flora interrupted.

"Who?" I asked, knowing full well Flora would burst if she didn't tell me.

"Gary Martin." Flora pressed her lips together as if she'd let slip a state secret. "And when I stopped to say hello, the first thing he mentioned was Mildred and Cyrus."

"Well, that's not surprising." I hated to disappoint my friend. "But that's pretty much what everyone is talking about these days. What with the skeleton, then Cyrus in a coma, throw in the Jacobs' family reunion and all these strangers in town," I made air quotes when I said the word strangers, "It's a wonder we're getting anything done. For our little town, that's a lot of action."

Flora nodded. "I know, but that's not what caught my attention. It's how he acted when he talked about them. He seemed, I don't know, too upset."

"Too upset? What do you mean?" Carter glanced up from the computer.

"He almost broke down into tears when he mentioned Mildred's name."

"I could see that," Carter said. "After all, he was accused of running off with the woman. It's clear at one time they were close. Maybe it's those sentiments that are coming into play here."

"Or relief his story has finally been proven true. That he hadn't run off with her or planned to, or whatever the rumors were back then," I added.

Flora leaned her elbow on the counter and placed her chin in her hand. "Most people thought Mildred moved to wherever Gary had gone, to be near him. That she never got over him and was still in love with him but didn't know how to break it to Cyrus. So, she took the easy route and left."

Carter's gray brows pulled into a tight V. "Wasn't he married?"

"Yes, but that's the thing. He headed to Texas alone," Flora said. "They'd been having problems."

"What kind of problems?" Carter asked.

"Didn't you say the wife was jealous? But for Mildred to follow a married man—that doesn't sound like her," I leaned my hip against the counter.

"Oh, we know from experience people do strange things. A woman in love might follow her heart and in turn, follow the one who holds her heart." Flora sighed. "Where do you think Shakespeare got all those ideas about love and love lost?"

"I figured he'd made them up." Carter grinned.

Flora blew out her protest. "Psh, men. No romance."

"Maureen would disagree with you. She thinks I'm very romantic." Carter winked, reminding me of his son, Gabe. "Speaking of romantic, Gabe is looking forward to your date Saturday night. He has something special planned. But I've been sworn to secrecy."

The knot of guilt in my stomach dislodged with his

words and dropped like lead to my feet. My face must've shown my thoughts because the smile on Carter's face faded.

"What is it, Amy Kate? You look like you swallowed a lemon, whole."

"I don't think I can go. Julia's family is still in town because of the assault, and I'd feel bad about abandoning her this weekend, even for an evening."

"From what I hear, it's going to be something special. I'd go so far as to say he's pulling out all the stops. Full works for a romantic evening."

What was I going to do? I could either be there for my friend, or I could spend the evening with a man I found amazing, fun, and a bully of a kisser.

The flash of the screen saver drew my eye to the computer in front of Carter.

I glanced over at the time. "I need to go, or the post office will close before I get there."

Grabbing my purse, I headed to the back workroom. Carter helped me load the boxes into my ancient blue van, and I maneuvered the few blocks to the post office.

As I stood in line waiting my turn, the picture of the young Gary Martin we had found in Mildred's jewelry box floated through my mind. Maybe Flora did pick up on something strange in her encounter with him. After all, Flora doesn't miss much, and I'd be foolish to dismiss her take on his behavior. No, she was the hub in the wheel of the Pine Lake community, and she'd know if one of the spokes was acting wonky.

Right then I decided to pay Gary Martin a visit first thing tomorrow.

A niggling thought that I should talk to Gabe about the date poked at my conscience. But before I could make any more life decisions, Ezra, the post clerk, called me to his window.

CHAPTER TWENTY

My text to Flora explained my plans for the morning and that I'd be in sometime in the afternoon. I wasn't worried. She'd been opening Twisted Plots since before it was Twisted Plots.

I googled Gary Martin's home address and set the maps app to guide me.

The mom-mobile rolled to a stop in front of an older home in the historical district of town. One of those bungalow types with a cement front porch, a colorful front door, and an old black iron fence with spikes that enclosed the front yard.

From my calculations and the information that Flora gave me, Gary Martin should be retired. At least, that's what I hoped.

I knocked on the door and a cacophony of yapping barks came from the other side.

"Get back, Harper. Now, Lee, get back," a female voice commanded.

The door inched open. All I could make out was a sliver of a nose, a piece of a chin, and one eye. It blinked against the morning sun. "Can I help you?"

"Hi. I'm Amy Kate Anderson."

"I'm sorry, Hon, but we don't give to door-to-door solicitors." The face pulled away from the crack, and the door moved forward.

I pushed against it. "No, I'm not selling anything. I'm looking for Gary Martin."

The door stopped, then opened fully. An older woman dressed in capri pants and a flowered tank top stepped out onto the porch. "Gary Martin? Why are you looking for him?"

"I needed to ask him some questions about Cyrus Jacobs. I suppose you heard he's in the hospital in a coma."

"I heard something about it." The woman gave me a hard stare. "Are you the cops?" She crossed her arms over her chest and raised her chin an inch.

"No, I'm not with the police. I'm a friend. Someone told me Gary had gone to see Cyrus the day of the attack."

"Well, if you think Gary had anything to do with it, you might as well put that out of your head. He's not the type. Wouldn't stand up to a cotton ball." A gleam of disdain sparked in her eyes. "Not like a real man. Some people never learn to fight for what's theirs."

Not sure where all this was going, I decided to backtrack a little. "Does Gary Martin live here?"

"Used to until about two months ago." She sighed and jammed her hands into her pockets. "But you can find him at the Whispering Pines Bed and Breakfast. He found a room closer to his office."

"Oh, I thought he'd be retired by now," I said.

A frown drew the wrinkles on her face tight. "You can't retire when you're up to your neck in debt." She pointed to the house behind her. "Nothing but a money pit. Between that and some bad investments, he'll be working two years after he dies. Give or take a year." The disdain in her eyes flooded over her face.

I noticed that she referred to the debt as his and his alone. For someone married to the guy, she didn't seem to claim his current circumstances as part of her own. "Can I ask you how long you've been married?"

Her eyes widened, and her laugh showed off her coffee-stained teeth. "Married? Oh, no, hon. I'm not married to that worthless windpipe. I'm his sister-in-law, Jess. Jess Roper. He's married to my sister, Trudy, though I tried to talk her out of it. Even back then, it was obvious he wasn't going to amount to anything. Tried to tell her." She tsked. "But what can you do? Now, they're living at the bed and breakfast until they can find something to rent."

"What about this house?" The math didn't add up for them to let the sister-in-law stay at their home if they were struggling like she said.

"Can't afford it anymore. So, I stepped in. I'm going to buy it from them. I hate the place, but Harper and Lee, my pugs, seem to like it, and I can't stand to see my little sister suffer because of his stupidity." She nodded and looked down at the black sandals on her feet. "Can't stand to see family in a spot. We've always been close. It's been the two of us for most of our lives, no one else."

I nodded my agreement. "I have two sisters of my own, so I get it."

"Yep, you do anything for family."

"Can you give me his work address?"

"Yeah, it's down on Lincoln Avenue, not far from the town square past the fire department."

We said our good-byes, and I slid back behind the steering wheel and headed for the town square. If the sister-in-law was right, I'd find Gary Martin at work.

But as I turned onto Lincoln Avenue, an idea presented itself, so I decided to go to Whispering Pines Bed and Breakfast instead.

The sister-in-law had painted quite the picture of Gary Martin. It didn't mesh with the information Flora provided. Maybe the wife could clear up the disconnect for me. Maybe meeting her would give me a better perspective of the man before I paid him a visit. After all, this was someone Mildred had cared about. I couldn't see her loving someone who was as worthless as Jess Roper made him out to be.

No, I needed more information before I met the man who possibly attacked Cyrus.

Trudy Martin met me at one of the tables by the windows in the café of the Whispering Pines Bed and Breakfast. The Whispering Pines had started serving lunch as well as breakfast several years back. My roommate, Julia, worked as their head chef for both shifts. Miles, her sous-chef, helped out.

Trudy differed greatly from the woman I'd met at the little bungalow. She wore a frilly feminine top, and her hair was cut in a short crop that framed her face perfectly. Wet, she might weigh a hundred pounds.

"Jess called and told me you'd stopped by." She slipped into the chair across from me.

The waitress flipped my coffee mug over and filled it to the rim. She did the same for Trudy. I inhaled the aroma and added the needed goodies.

"I figured you'd go see Gary at the office. It surprised me when the desk clerk called up to let me know you were here." Her southern drawl added to her femininity.

"I wondered if you could tell me what Gary was doing at Cyrus's house Saturday morning."

"I have no idea. I thought he'd gone for a walk or maybe to the office. I didn't know he was even thinking of going to see Cyrus until he returned, and then later that day, we heard about the attack. Guess I should've known he couldn't stay away."

"What do you mean?" I asked.

"Mildred. The minute I heard they'd found her remains I knew he'd get mixed up in it." She shook her head and leaned back against the chair. The lace on her blouse swayed as she adjusted in her seat.

I stirred my coffee wondering how to ask if her husband was still in love with Mildred Jacobs. As it turned out, I didn't have to ask.

"He never got over her." She sighed, then leaned her elbows on the table and drew closer to me.

I leaned in as well, shortening the distance between us as if we were two old friends sharing a secret.

"If you ask me, he simply couldn't let go of her. Even after—" The expression on her face hardened.

"Even after what?" My eyes met hers.

"You know, when she disappeared."

"I guess that affected your marriage. How did you feel about Mildred?" I asked.

"I didn't feel anything. I'm the one he married." She leaned back again, breaking the connection.

"Yes, but I was told that when Gary moved to Texas he went alone. What happened?" I picked up my mug and took a sip.

"You don't mince words, do you?" Trudy played with the spoon beside her coffee cup. She studied me for a moment, then crossed her legs, and tilted her head to one side. "Why should I talk to you about this? You're not the police, right?" The spoon stilled, and she placed it on the table beside her mug. "No, I'm done here. I want to leave the past in the past, but I knew the instant I heard about Mildred and that road crew, she'd found a way to hurt my marriage even from beyond the grave." She stood. "I'll let you discuss this with Gary. He can tell you why he left for Texas alone. But it's not what you and everybody else thinks." Her hand shot to her chest. "I won't allow myself to be cross-examined over something that happened thirty years ago. And as far as what happened Saturday, you'll have to talk to Gary. He's the one who should have to answer for his actions, not me."

She moved to leave, but I touched her arm. "Trudy, I

didn't mean to upset you. I just thought maybe you could help me find Mildred's killer by shedding some light on who might have wanted to hurt her. You were here in Pine Lake during the late eighties. Who would've wanted to do such a thing?"

Jerking her arm from my hand, she glared at me. "I have no idea. Why don't you go ask those goody two-shoes she used to hang out with over at Pine Lake First Church?" She sashayed past me, then called over her shoulder, "But don't be fooled. Those women come across as kind and caring, but when threatened, the claws come out."

She stormed off toward the lobby of the inn, dodging tables on her way out the door. I motioned to the waitress for the bill. I thought about Trudy Martin and her sister, Jess. Polar opposites in appearance. Jess strong and fierce while Trudy the epitome of soft femininity, but they weren't that different. Below the surface they were both strong-minded women, capable of standing up for what was theirs.

CHAPTER TWENTY-ONE

With freshly painted fingernails, Gary Martin's receptionist waved me on through.

Gary sat behind his desk, a phone to his ear, and when I tapped on his open door, he beckoned me into the room. He grunted a few 'uh-huhs' into the phone he held. I took a seat across from him in one a steel-framed, cloth chair.

"I've got to go. Yeah, yeah. I'll let you know the minute I know. No, you don't have to call back tomorrow. No, I'll call you when I find out." A smile played on his lips, and his eyes met mine. "Yes, Mrs. Jenkins. I'll be sure to do that. Yes, thank you." He hung up the receiver and sighed. "Mrs. Jenkins. I hear from her about twice a day concerning her pending lawsuit. Poor old dear, it's all she has to occupy her mind."

I nodded. "That happens when you're waiting on something. It can consume you."

"Yes. Now how may I help you? Miss ..."

"Amy Kate Anderson, I'm here to talk to you about Cyrus Jacobs." I crossed my legs and settled my purse in the chair beside me. "I've been asked by Cyrus's niece to look into the attack on him. It came to my attention that you had visited him last Saturday morning. I'm assuming before the attack."

"Yes, the police have already been here and questioned me about it."

"Would you mind going over what happened again? I'd like to help Julia and the Jacobs if I can."

"Sure." Gary shrugged. "As I told the detective, I went to see Cyrus to check on him. I figured he'd be upset about finding Mildred's remains, and I wanted to offer him my condolences." A wave of pain crossed his face. The playful gleam that had been in his eyes moments before faded, replaced with a shadow of grief. Even his shoulders sagged as he spoke her name. "Mildred was such a gentle soul. So kind and forgiving. I can't imagine who would've done such a thing to her."

"So, you thought she'd run off then? Just gone away without saying good-bye to Cyrus?" I asked.

Gary shook his head. "To be honest, I didn't know what to think. She came to my house earlier that same week to tell me good-bye because I was moving to Houston. When I found out that she'd gone missing, I couldn't imagine her just up and leaving. She loved Cyrus."

"So, the rumors weren't true that something was going on between you?" I tilted my head to one side, studying him, watching to see if his answers rang true.

"No, they weren't. I'd been offered a job with a firm there, and frankly, I needed to get out of Pine Lake. Too many memories, and the people here were having a hard time letting go of things."

"Like what exactly?"

His jaw tightened. "Like letting people move on with their lives. Mildred married Cyrus. I married Trudy. But everyone in town kept bringing up our relationship. So much so that Trudy wanted to call it quits."

"Is that why you went to Houston alone, then?"

"Boy, you've done your homework. How do you know all this?" Gary's brows furrowed, and he crossed his arms on his desk. "Never mind. I have an idea how you've come by your information." He looked down at the files under his elbows. "I went to Houston alone to get settled. Trudy and I needed some time apart, and this way, I could find us an apartment and start the new job without putting her through that. She was going to handle selling the house here."

"So, you and Trudy took a break from your marriage. Is that right?"

"No, not our marriage. There was never a question about the marriage. We needed some time apart to sort things out."

"What things? Mildred?"

Gary squirmed in his seat and played with the corner of one of the file folders on his desk. "Look, I won't deny I had feelings for her. She was kind and had a way about her that set everyone at ease. But she married Cyrus, and once she did, I moved on. Then I met Trudy and couldn't have been happier."

"So happy you needed time apart." The words slipped out before I could stop them.

"Miss Anderson, is it? I don't appreciate a complete stranger coming into my office and grilling me about something that, to be perfectly frank, is none of their business. Now, do you have any questions for me about last Saturday, or are we done?" His cool stare sent chills cascading over me. But Anderson women are made of Southern iron, and I wasn't going to let some two-bit lawyer with a big vocabulary bully me, even if he was right.

"Last Saturday, when you saw Cyrus, how did he act? Did he seem upset or worried?"

"Only about what had happened. About finding Mildred. But not worried. Why?"

"I have reason to believe that he discovered something about his family that might have worried him. Did he mention anything about the family reunion or being agitated with any of his family members?"

Gary Martin leaned back in his chair, his face turning ash white.

"Are you all right? What is it?" I scooted to the edge of my chair in case I needed to rush to perform some lifesaving feat. My outdated CPR certification card flashed before my eyes.

"Mildred. I remember Mildred mentioning to me that she'd been worried about someone in Cyrus's family. The day she came to say good-bye. She'd been anxious, and I'd asked her if she planned on going to the women's retreat that weekend."

I pressed my lips together, not wanting to interrupt.

"I thought she might be upset with one of the other ladies, but she said no, she was worried about a family issue. But then Mildred said she knew how to help." Gary looked over at me. "That was so like her. Always trying to help."

"It's nice that you have good memories of her." My grief counseling came from my own experiences concerning the death of my mom. People often think that you grieve and then it passes, but anyone who's gone through a loss knows that grief is like the ocean. The waves wash in then out of your life, leaving their mark along the shore, coming and going with fair regularity.

My heart felt for this man who had once loved this woman. I stood to take my leave, but before I reached the door, Gary spoke, "She was such a lovely person. I never understood how she could have become friends with Kelly and Beth after the way they'd treated her the first year she and Cyrus were married." His gaze met mine. "I'd talk to Beth. Kelly moved out of town before Trudy and I moved back, but maybe Beth can shed some light on what happened that day."

"Any idea where I can find her?" I asked.

"Yeah, last I heard, Beth Jackson works as the church secretary at First Church." He flipped his wrist over and looked at the time. "If you hurry, you might catch her before lunch. But as for last Saturday, when I left Cyrus, he was fine. He had his shovel propped by the back door ready to do some work in his orchard."

I froze. "Did you happen to see any jars sitting around?"

Gary's brows pulled together, making jumbled lines appear on his forehead. "As a matter of fact, there were a couple of jars with paper in them sitting on the floor by the back door."

"Was the paper green?" It took everything in me not to say more.

"No, it was yellowed with lines. Maybe, old notebook paper."

CHAPTER TWENTY-TWO

So, yellowed paper filled the pickle jars, not money.

My mind whirled as I slipped into the driver seat of my minivan and revved the engine, so it would stay running. The crazy thing had started acting up. I turned the mom mobile toward First Church. Beth Jackson was next on my list.

I skidded around the corner onto Harding Street and mulled over the new information I'd received from Gary Martin. Had Cyrus been burying the letters when he was attacked? Maybe. Everything pointed to Carol White and those letters she swore she didn't write. And now were missing. Hard to prove that she wrote them if you couldn't find them.

I passed through the stop sign without seeing it.

No matter how I arranged the puzzle pieces of this case, only small sections connected.

The car in front of me stopped, and I glanced up in time to see the rear lights flash red. I slammed on the brakes, thankful that someone was looking out for me.

As I waited at the light, I ticked off the facts of the case that were true. Someone broke into Uncle Cyrus's house and dug up some of the jars in his orchard. The letters that he possessed on Friday were gone Saturday. Only a handful of people knew about the letters. Carol was the only one who had read any of them. Well, besides the one that I borrowed from Uncle Cyrus's library. Okay, took.

Then there was the second assailant. Fast and thin. No way was it Percy White. Honestly, he couldn't move that fast. So, who was the second assailant, and how did he fit into the picture?

The lanky body of the oily teen popped into my mind. He'd be the right size, but he wouldn't be able to keep that kind of information to himself. The guy would want to brag about his exploits. Perhaps tonight I'll ply him with pizza and quiz him. He might take the bait if I'm subtle enough.

Three car horns blared in alternating blasts to let me know the light had turned.

I pulled into the parking space closest to the steps in the back of the church and checked the time on the dashboard before turning off the engine. Eleven o'clock. Hopefully, Beth would still be here.

The office of First Church radiated a blue hue. Blue walls, blue carpet, blue padded chairs. I swear even the little old lady who greeted me had blue hair. I bit the inside of my cheek to keep from laughing.

The woman looked up from the screen in front of her, her glasses perched at the end of her nose. She looked at me more over her glasses than through them. "Can I help you, dear?" she asked.

"I'm looking for Beth Jackson. I understand she works here."

"Yes, she stepped out for a minute, but it shouldn't be long." She pointed to the blue padded chairs, and I took a seat.

A few minutes later, a tall slender woman of about sixty entered the room, carrying a clipboard. "Richard said to let him know the instant the other men arrive. He's anxious to settle this matter as soon as possible." The woman walked to the end of the counter and unlatched the little wooden swinging door that separated the workers from the public.

"You have someone waiting for you, Beth." The older woman nodded in my direction without lifting her hands from the keyboard.

Beth turned towards me, and I stood and moved to the counter.

"How can I help you?" She leaned her elbows on the counter, shrinking her size somewhat.

"I'm Amy Kate Anderson. Is there any way I could speak to you about Mildred Jacobs?"

The woman's countenance grew dark, and she straightened to her full height. "Oh." She looked around, then gestured towards a room behind the counter. "Let's use James's office. He won't mind, and then we won't disturb anyone."

I suspected Beth was more concerned about being overheard by a certain blue-haired woman than disturbing others.

She waited for me to enter the room, then shut the door behind us. I took a seat in another blue padded chairs that seemed to grow out of the church's floor like weeds, and she sat in the rolling black chair behind the desk.

"I'd heard that they'd found Mildred's body." She pressed her lips together and shook her head. "It's terrible."

"That's why I'm looking into it for Julia, her niece. It has Cyrus and the whole Jacobs' family so upset."

"I can only imagine. What can I do for you?"

"It would help if you could tell me what happened that week, the week she went missing. Cyrus said she was supposed to go to a women's retreat with some of you ladies here in the church. That she had planned to ride with you and Kelly Parnell."

"That's right. But she'd called me earlier in the week

and said she might not go, that something had come up. I told her not to make up her mind yet. To wait and see what happened. Then when I didn't hear from her, Kelly and I thought she'd decided not to go." She clasped her hands together on the desk. "You could've knocked me over with a feather when Cyrus called me up that Sunday night asking where Mildred was."

"How did he seem to you?"

"Worried, out of his mind—that's how he seemed." Her eyes softened as she spoke of Cyrus. "He loved her so much."

"That's what everyone keeps telling me. Do you know why she thought about skipping the retreat?"

Beth stared past me; her gaze fixed on a spot behind me. "Something about a family matter. I think. It's been so long." Under her breath, she whispered, "Thirty years." Then she shook her head again.

"You might want to talk to Gary Martin. They were an item once. Maybe, he could help you."

"I've been to see him. Funny thing. He sent me to see you, as did his wife."

She raised her eyebrows. "Well then, there's not much more I can tell you. She thought about going but didn't." She shrugged and rolled the chair back from the desk.

"Do you happen to have Kelly Parnell's phone number. I'd like to talk to her, see if she has anything to add."

"Let me jot it down for you." Beth pulled open the middle drawer of the desk and fished out a sticky note pad. When she finished, she stood and handed me the paper.

I didn't budge. "I understand that when Cyrus and Mildred first married, things were tense between the two of you. Can you tell me what that was about?"

Her cold look set off my warning bells.

"Let's just say that several hearts were broken when Cyrus announced his intentions to marry Mildred. After all, he'd been one of Pine Lake's most eligible bachelors for a long time. Then when he married someone younger, almost fifteen years his junior, it didn't go over well with the town's single females."

"Were you one of the brokenhearted?" I asked.

Beth circled the desk and opened the door. "It's better for everyone if we leave the past in the past. Don't you think?"

The June afternoon heat rushed over me when I returned from the postal run. It didn't take as long now since the schools were out for the summer, but the air conditioner in my van didn't have time to get cranking with the cool air. The sweat trickled down my back.

I pulled into the parking space to the side of Twisted Plots and sat debating whether I should go tell Gabe now that I'd need to cancel our date or wait another day or two to see if anything changed. It was doubtful that we'd catch Cyrus's assailants and Mildred's murderer by Saturday, but who knew?

Carter had commented several times over the last two days about how much Gabe was looking forward to Saturday night. That he'd gone all out. A heavy sigh escaped from my lips. I couldn't avoid it forever.

He'll understand, I told myself, stepping out of the van and heading toward the police station. Maybe, he won't be there. Maybe, he's busy and won't see me. Maybe ...

But before I got to my next maybe, I heard Gabe's voice calling from the direction of Twisted Plots. "Hey, where are you going?" He jogged up beside me on the town green.

"I was headed over to see you," I said.

Gabe's brown eyes gleamed. "Couldn't stay away, huh?" A half-grin appeared on his lips, and he raised an eyebrow.

"Yeah, if I don't get my daily dose of Gabe the Babe, I

can't function." I laid the back of my hand across my forehead. "Oh, I feel faint even now." I teetered and fell in his direction.

Out of instinct, he caught me. "I should've let you fall for calling me Gabe the Babe. What is that? Some kind of nickname you gave me?"

"Oh, please. Don't tell me you haven't heard that one before. Half the women in town call you that."

He scowled and set me back on my feet.

"Don't be that way. It's a compliment. Plus, you brought it on yourself."

"How?" He asked.

"By driving that shiny, red Corvette. And don't tell me you drive it for the gas mileage."

He shrugged, and a hint of mischief played in his warm eyes. "It's a classic. So, why were you looking for me?"

I took a step back. His presence in my personal space made it hard for me to think, especially when he stood so close, I could smell the musk droplets in his cologne. "I need to cancel our plans for Saturday night," I blurted out. "I know you told me to circle the date, but Danny being at the apartment is my fault. My conscience won't let me go out with you while my best friend is struggling to keep all her relatives happy and coping with Cyrus."

His jaw tightened, but he nodded his understanding.

"I'm sorry. I can't leave Julia in a lurch."

"It's okay. I understand. After I thought about it, I realized I was making you choose, and I don't want to do that. It's just that for the last few months, we can't seem to connect. Between my job and your business and our families, we don't ever get a chance to spend time together, alone."

"You're right, and the minute the Jacobs' crew leaves town, I'm yours."

Gabe stuck his hands in his pants pockets.

"What?" I slid my hand through the crook of his arm

and gave him a slight hip bump.

"Are you sure you want to do this? It seems like there's always an excuse. I mean if we're surrounded by family or catching lunch with others, it's fine, but I think you're afraid of what this could be."

Shocked, I let go of his arm. "If I recall correctly, you've called off as many dates as I have. Remember our date to go to Hooks, just the two of us, and you cancelled because of a case. Then there was the time we were supposed to go to the opening night of that play, and you couldn't make it because of your brother, Michael, and his car wreck. Then there was the night we'd planned to go—"

"Okay, okay. You've made your point. It's not all you. Sorry." He grabbed my hand and intertwined our fingers. "I was just looking forward to having you all to myself."

I ran my finger down his jaw and placed my hand on his cheek. "I know. I was looking forward to it too, but I'm the reason Danny is at our apartment, and I hate to stick Julia with dealing with him all weekend on her own." I patted his cheek. "You could solve the case, though, and send them on their merry way. Then I wouldn't have any excuses, and I'd be free to galivant with you on our mystery date."

He wrapped his hand over mine, pulled it to his lips, and placed a kiss on it.

Tingling sensations ran all over me and a stupid grin spread across my face. The man knew how to make my heart race.

Someone whistled, and I peered over toward the bookshop. Carter stood outside by the window, waving.

Heat crept up my cheeks, and I dropped my hand to my side. I'd forgotten we were standing in the middle of the town green for all the world to see. That's what Gabe Cooper did to me. He made me forget everyone else in the world but him.

Gabe waved to his father and grinned at me. "So, I was

looking for you to find out if you'd come up with anything? Since you did agree to report any new information and not go off on your own."

We watched Carter step back inside the store.

"I remember our agreement. Well, I did go see Gary Martin. I didn't get much from him. Seems in spite of the rumors floating around town at the time, there wasn't anything going on between him and Mildred. No, everyone swears she was devoted to Cyrus."

"That's what he told me, too. And the two women that she was supposed to go to the retreat with said the same thing, that Mildred would never have cheated on Cyrus and that she loved him."

So, Gabe had contacted Kelly Parnell. I'd have to make my own phone call this afternoon. Maybe, she'd be more open with someone who wasn't a cop.

Gabe took a step toward the bookshop. "Come on. I'll walk you over." He took my hand, and we retraced our steps. "How's your house guest? Is he behaving himself?"

The encounter with him in the van and his brazen attitude flashed through my thoughts. "He's fine. Why?"

"We received a complaint about vandalism, and the officer on duty said that the group of teenagers he'd interviewed were mouthy, but he couldn't prove they were the ones who'd committed the vandalism. I went around to get statements from the campers who'd called it in," Gabe said. "From the descriptions the eyewitnesses gave, Danny was one of them."

"Interesting. Have you had any time to check out Percy White since I told you about his gambling habit?"

"Yes, he's been in a spot of trouble here and there through the years. Nothing that stuck. But some of it did have connections to his gambling. Which means if he still has a gambling problem, he'd have motive for attacking Cyrus. Since Cyrus mentioned to Carol about the pickle jars buried in the orchard, it wouldn't be a stretch to assume she told Percy about them."

I nodded. "I hate to say it, but the kid was there, too when Cyrus mentioned the jars."

Gabe looked down at the sidewalk and then back at me. "It breaks my heart to see a kid go sideways. It's the part of the job I hate. Especially when it could've been avoided."

"I know." I levered up on my toes and kissed his cheek. "And that's why you're my superhero."

"No," he laughed. "That's why I'm Gabe the Babe."

"Don't get too full of yourself." I lowered my heels back to the ground.

He winked at me. "Like you said, it's not my fault. I blame it on the car."

CHAPTER TWENTY-THREE

The aroma wafting from the kitchen made my mouth water. I hung my purse on the empty coat rack behind the front door and kicked off my red high heel shoes.

"Hey, that you?" Julia called over the clanking noise of what I hoped were pots full of something delicious.

Since the reunion, Julia hadn't cooked much at the apartment. I didn't blame her, but this was a nice surprise. No need to ply the teenager with pizza. By the smell of whatever Julia had cooking, it would do the trick.

"Yeah, it's me. Where is our house guest?" I asked, plopping into one of the overstuffed chairs. My toes ached from all the shelving of inventory today. Tuesdays were always like that at the bookshop. Monday deliveries, Tuesday shelving inventory, Wednesdays praying for customers, so we could do it all again the following week. A smile rose to my lips. How I loved my bookshop.

Julia stuck her head around the door frame. "He's taking a shower, getting cleaned up for dinner."

"Did you hear the police interrogated him today?"

Julia wiped her hands on the dish towel that hung from her apron pocket. "About Uncle Cyrus?"

"No, about some vandalism down at the campgrounds.

Apparently, some teenagers were throwing rocks at the streetlights in the parking lot and painted some bad words on a few of the canoes."

"That's not good." Julia stepped into the room and glanced down the hall toward the bathroom. "Is it wise to have him here?"

"No, but because of me and my big mouth, we're stuck." I leaned back in the chair and stretched my legs out in front of me and wiggled my toes. Gizmo appeared from down the hall and jumped into my lap. Oh, it felt good to be home.

"Maybe not. Maybe we could suggest to Carol that we're not fit to supervise him. Blame it on our lack of experience with teenagers. Tell her he's only been with us a day and half and he's already in trouble."

I met Julia's gaze. "This isn't Danny's first time being in trouble with the law. He has a bit of a rap sheet."

"What?" Julia's voice rose an octave or two. Then in a whisper, she asked, "Are you serious? He's a criminal? Amy Kate, he has to go. Blood or no blood. He's out of here."

"Fine. But you do remember he's your kinfolk, not mine."

"Yes, but you're the one who invited him into our home." Julia flung the dish towel over her left shoulder and crossed her arms. "And you are the one who's going to uninvite him." Julia turned and disappeared into the kitchen.

I heard the bathroom door open and the squish, squish, squish of the carpet as Danny made his way down the hall to the living room.

"Hey," I said. Gizmo groaned at the teen.

Danny lifted his chin in a slight nod. If I'd looked away, I'd have missed it.

His black hair hung wet, dripping into a white towel around his neck. He was bare chested and wore a pair of basketball shorts that drooped to his knees. When he leaned over to put his clothes into his backpack, something dropped out of his pocket next to my chair. Danny didn't notice, so I scooted forward with Gizmo in my arms and picked up the oblong object. It was a knife. The initials D.J.W. were carved into the bone handle. I ran my hand over the smooth surface. "Nice knife." I held it out to him.

He looked up from the backpack and took it. "Oh, I must've dropped it."

"Yeah, it fell out of your pocket. You might want to be more careful with it. You don't want to lose it. It looks expensive."

"It was a Christmas gift from my dad last year." He clutched it in his fist. "He gave one to me and one to my brother David. Dave said it's made from ivory tusk. But I don't think that's true. You never know with David." Danny put the knife back into the same pocket. Then pulling a dark tee-shirt from his bag, he slipped it on over his head.

"Well, be careful then. It would be a shame for you to lose it." I carried Gizmo into the kitchen to see if Julia needed my help. Plus, I wanted to chat with her about my phone call with Kelly Parnell. She'd said the same thing Beth had said, Mildred hadn't gone with them and she didn't know why.

Seated around the table, the three of us kept the conversation light and unimportant. Sheer drivel. The kid didn't want to talk about his family, and the few times I tried to steer the conversation in that direction, he clammed up.

The only success I had in pulling any information from the oily teen happened when I mentioned the family grill-off. Percy White had won the thing. "So, I bet your dad was excited to win. He sure looked like he knew a thing or two about grilling when I stopped to talk to him."

"Yeah, he was happy about it. I mean it's hard to tell

with him," Danny said.

"What do you mean? Doesn't he show much excitement?"

"No, he didn't expect to win. He didn't have all his usual ingredients, so he didn't think he'd do very well." Danny took a bite and waved the empty fork around while he talked. "He and David went to the store that morning, but when they got back, they didn't have any of the seasonings and stuff. Dad said he couldn't find them in the local store."

I shot a look at Julia, whose eyes widened. "So, your dad wasn't with you and your mom Saturday morning? He and your brother David went to the supermarket."

"Yeah, that's right."

"Did you notice if they were carrying any bags when they returned?"

"Why would they, if they couldn't find what they went for?" Danny frowned. "But yes, he had bags because he bought the meat."

I recognized the lie the instant it stood up and shouted at me. Carol had told me and Cyrus Friday afternoon that Percy was out buying the meat. There is no way he'd make two trips. And it wouldn't surprise me one iota to find out Percy won because he did have all his spices. That he'd used his sweet southern hot sauce as an excuse to get away from the campgrounds, Saturday morning.

Danny must've realized his mistake.

"So, is David still in town. I haven't met him yet."

Julia took a sip of her tea and placed the glass on the table. "Now that you mention it, I saw him passing through the buffet line Friday at the luncheon."

"Oh, so what does he look like? I mean, does he look like your dad or more like you?" I directed my question to Danny.

He squinted his eyes and gave me a hard stare. "You're starting to sound like a cop. Maybe you've been hanging around your boyfriend too long."

I sat ramrod straight in my chair. "How do you know I have a boyfriend?"

"You told me, remember? In that death-inspiring car ride, and besides, I saw you in the town square earlier today with him."

"How do you know the guy she was with was a cop? He could've been a real estate agent for all you know." Julia asked, even though she already knew the answer.

"Because he asked me questions about some graffiti in the campground." He scooted his chair out from under the table and stood. "I'm full. Can I watch some TV?"

"After you clear your place. Put your dishes in the sink, and one of us will take care of them," I said.

After Danny left the room, Julia sighed and rolled her shoulders. "If this is parenting, I'm never having children."

"Don't say that, Jules. You'll make a great mom. Look at the practice you've had taking care of me." I laughed.

"True."

"Speaking of taking care of me, how would you feel about a little adventure?"

A spark appeared in Julia's eyes. "What kind of adventure are we talking about?"

"The kind where we break a few laws and hope not to get caught."

"Ooh, my favorite." Julia giggled. "Does that mean I get to wear my army-secret agent- commando chick outfit?"

"Of course. Black is the chic look for trespassing."

"I'm sure I'll regret this, but count me in." Julia leaned her elbow on the table and pulled her chair closer to me. "So, what's the plan?"

The stars shone bright against the black canopy of the sky, and the early June moon hung high like a spectator in a balcony seat at a concert. The heat had lifted, and a warm gentle breeze tiptoed through the leaves of the trees in the orchard, causing the shadows on the ground to sway.

I clung tight to my flashlight and fought the urge to jump at every sound. Julia's breath on the back of my neck made me shudder. "Julia, be careful. Don't step on me."

"It's so creepy out here. And what are all those noises? I expected peace and quiet in the middle of the night this far out of town."

The light from her flashlight melted into mine. "Shine your light to the right, and I'll keep mine on the ground in front of us. Remember, we're looking for the holes where we found the shovels and the blood. I'm sure that's where Cyrus buried the letters."

"Fine. I'll take the right. But you owe me big time for this."

We walked along, sweeping our lights across the ground as we went deeper into the orchard. It hadn't seemed like the area was this far from the house the other day. Maybe coming at midnight was a mistake, but I didn't want anyone else, especially a certain lieutenant, to spot us out here looking around. I needed to find the letters first before telling Gabe about them being buried.

"Shouldn't the area be roped off or something? After all it's a crime scene, right?" Julia asked in my ear.

"Yeah, there should be something."

"Are you sure we went down the right row? With this many apple trees in the dark, we could've picked the wrong one," Julia asked.

"Let's go a few more feet, and if we don't see anything, we'll go back." I huffed. She was right. In the dark, I couldn't tell one row of apple trees from another, and neither could she.

After exploring four rows without success, I didn't hold out much hope for finding the area. I thought about giving up, but the contents of the letters drew me.

Julia veered to the right not far behind me. We both

relaxed, and the chirping of the insects and the occasional hooting of an owl no longer set off my flight instinct.

I was just about to suggest we try the next row when a thud followed by a groan came from Julia's direction and the beam from her flashlight swirled around on the ground like a spinning top. I whirled around and hurried back. "Julia?"

"Over here," she called.

I found her sitting on the ground holding her ankle.

"Oh, no."

"Sorry." Julia took my hand, and I helped her to her feet. "I stepped on some apples and slipped."

"Should we head back and forget it?" I didn't want to make her injury worse by dragging her up and down a million more rows of apple trees.

She pressed her foot to the ground and took a few steps. "No, it's not serious. It should be all right." Julia leaned over and picked up her flashlight.

When she did, the beam of light reflected off a strand of yellow crime tape.

"Look." I pointed to the bright yellow.

"Finally." Julia sighed.

I ducked under the tape, but Julia stood outside it, facing the house, watching. I wasn't sure if Gabe was still having a patrol car cruise by the house or not. There hadn't been anyone parked in the driveway when we came up, but I'd parked behind the house to be safe.

Swinging my flashlight over the area, I counted seven holes within the boundaries of the tape, then moved from one hole to another, shining my light into the depths of each one and running my hand across the bottom of them.

I shivered each time my hand landed on a new type of bug. The night crawlers were the worst. Among the bugs, I found a few pop tops, a penny, a pocketknife, and two candy wrappers. The penny and the pocketknife I shoved into the front pocket of my black jeans. I'd gone commando chick all the way.

At one hole, my beam bounced off something dingy white. Another wrapper, no doubt. Sticking my hand into the hole, I retrieved a shred of paper. I put it under the beam to examine it. To my delight, I held a torn corner of an envelope. Yes, at one time the letters had been here. Gary Martin was telling the truth.

If I was right, Cyrus was out here burying the letters when he was attacked. But why had his assailants moved him to the library?

"Did you find something?" Julia called over her shoulder.

"Yeah, a torn piece of an envelope."

"That's great. That means the letters have been here, and whoever attacked Uncle Cyrus has the letters."

I groaned.

"What?" Julia turned her flashlight on me.

I raised my arm to shield my eyes, and she lowered the beam. "If they took the letters, then more than likely they destroyed them."

"What makes you say that?" Julia asked.

"Because they didn't dig up any of the other rows." I shined my flashlight back on the piece of paper in my hand. There were a couple of marks I could make out, but they looked different from the ones in the letter I'd read. The swirl of the S was distinctive on the letter from Carol. This one was fatter, not as sleek.

"I'm not following." Julia lifted the tape and joined me.

"If they'd been looking for money, they would've dug all over."

"Maybe you interrupted them. You did say you surprised the guy in the house," Julia said.

"True, but I don't think that's why they were here. Remember, the jar we found full of money was still buried. Gabe had to wrestle it loose from the dirt. I think they came for the letters. That's why the library was torn apart."

"That's possible. But why do you think they wanted the letters?"

"They wanted the letters because they incriminated the writer in some way." I met Julia's gaze. "The letters might hold the answer to Mildred's murder."

"If they're destroyed, what are we going to do?" Julia asked.

"Let's go check the library again. Maybe Uncle Cyrus and the assailants missed something. I mean those letters must've been tucked away in several books, and there must've been a lot of them, since Uncle Cyrus dug seven holes. Surely, they didn't find them all."

"Yeah, it's worth a try."

We headed toward the house, Julia taking the lead, careful not to make any noise. A seriousness about the work settled over me. I wanted to catch Mildred's killer, not just for Julia but for Cyrus. He'd been through so much, and it pained me to think of him lying in a hospital bed in a coma. Cyrus needed justice, and I wanted to give it to him.

As we neared the house, I caught sight of a flash of movement to my right among the trees.

"Julia," I whispered.

She stopped, I grabbed her forearm, and we turned off our flashlights. The moonlight threw everything into shades of gray and black. We stood frozen, listening.

All I heard was the croaking of the frogs in the back pond, the swish of the leaves in the trees, and the motor of a car. I pulled Julia into the shadows of the nearest tree and leaned against the hard trunk.

A twig snapped.

Julia's eyes grew to the size of teacup saucers.

I peeked around the tree in the direction of the noise. A shadow moved between two trees across the narrow footpath. The black form headed our way.

"What did you see?" Julia whispered.

"There's someone out there, and I don't think it's the police."

"That's not good. I can handle the police. I'm not prepared to meet a killer," she squeaked.

"Come on." I grabbed her hand and shot out from behind the tree, not caring who heard us. There was no way I was waiting around to find out the identity of the shadowy figure. Not with the car sitting maybe fifty feet away.

Julia ran full speed, her arms pumping at her sides. I followed close behind her. Footsteps sounded behind me, hitting the ground quick, one thud after the other.

Glancing over my shoulder, I screamed.

A hand flew over my mouth and dragged me to the ground. "Hush."

I recognized the voice. Anger ignited in me, and I threw an elbow into his ribs for good measure. "Get off me."

Julia stopped midstride and turned and tackled the guy. Swinging her arm above her head, she held her flashlight like a club.

He hit the ground and scrambled to his feet. "Stop. It's me," he hissed.

For a minute, it looked like Julia's head would explode. "Do you know how close you were to getting clobbered?" She lowered her arm.

He put his finger to his lips. "Shh ... Be quiet." He ducked back into the tree line, dragging me with him. I snatched Julia's hand, and the three of us scrambled back into the shadows.

"Chet Baker. I ought to—"

"Now, Amy Kate, I know all about your temper. I'm the good guy here."

"Good guy?" Julia said.

"Keep it down." Chet motioned with his hands for us to lower our voices. "There are some thugs up at the house. They showed up a few minutes ago. I didn't want you to run into them. Especially if they're the ones who got to Cyrus."

"What are you doing here?"

Chet chuckled. "I've been watching you since you arrived. One of my sources told me they heard some guys talking out at the campgrounds earlier today. Said one referred to pickle jars and a map." Chet shrugged. "It didn't take a genius to figure out what they were discussing."

"I didn't see any cars when I drove up. Where'd you park?" Amy Kate asked.

"Over by the road construction equipment. I brought a truck, so it blended in. Didn't want the police to know I was here." He scowled. "You, however, announced your presence to the world. I'm surprised the two goons haven't come looking for you yet." Chet glanced toward the house. "We'd better go somewhere a little safer. It won't be long before they show up."

"Maybe they'll think the van is Cyrus's," Julia added.

"Let's hope so," Chet said. "Meanwhile, we need to go somewhere out of sight. I have a feeling once they find the map in the library, their plan is to do a little digging in the orchard."

"Why do you think that?" I asked.

"Because according to my source, these hoodlums wanted to break some guy's legs today, and in order to save his neck, he gave up Cyrus's stash."

"You mean there's a map?" Julia asked.

CHAPTER TWENTY-FOUR

Chet scooted closer to me to give Julia more room behind the woodpile. It was close to the house and wide enough for the three of us to fit behind. Plus, it gave us a great view of the back door where, according to Chet, the two goons had entered.

"I watched them get out. They seemed nervous," Chet said.

"Do you think we should stop them?" Julia whispered. "I can't sit here and let them take all of Uncle Cyrus's money."

"Do you really think there are pickle jars full of money out in the orchard?" Chet asked.

Neither Julia nor I answered the question.

Before I could balance on my knees, the back door swung open and a man emerged, descending the steps two at a time, headed to the car. "I'm bringing him in and turning off the car," he shouted over his shoulder, then mumbled, "Idiot. Who leaves the air running for a mark?"

The man walked around the car and tried to slide into the driver's seat. The steering wheel stopped him. Reaching down, he pushed the seat further back.

Someone or something yelped.

"Shut up. I'll deal with you in a minute," the man

snarled. Cutting the engine, he grabbed the keys and stood, tucking them into his pocket. Then he threw open the back door and pulled another rather large man from the depths of the car.

Julia gasped. Percy White emerged, hands tied behind his back and a swatch of gray duct tape plastered across his mouth.

I looked at Julia and then at Chet, who shrugged and placed his finger to his lips. We ducked lower behind the woodpile.

Chet stretched his leg to the side, looking like a lopsided tripod, and dug in his G-star designer jean's pocket for his phone.

"What are you doing?" I whispered to Chet.

Julia peeked over the top of the woodpile. "They're standing at the bottom of the steps." She took another quick glance. "I don't think they know we're here."

"I'm calling the police. They've got someone tied up and gagged," Chet said.

"Yeah, but if we call the cops, we'll never find out if there are any more letters. Besides, they could arrest us for tampering with a crime scene."

Chet smirked. "Right. Like Lieutenant Red Corvette is going to arrest you, his best girl. Fat chance."

"I'm not his best girl." My voice rose. Julia and Chet shushed me and waved their hands for me to quiet down. I bit off my words and turned my attention back to the two men standing by the steps.

The one dragged Percy by the arm up the stairs to the porch. The back door opened and a shaft of light leaked out from the kitchen. A slim gentleman poked his head through the opening. "What are you doing with him?"

"I can't leave him in the car. Finding that map is taking forever in that mess, and he's liable to try and escape," the large man said. "Maybe he can help. Maybe he knows more than he's saying."

"Okay. It did take some doing to convince him to tell us about the map." The slim man stepped back into the house, and the large one shoved Percy through the doorway. The light from the house disappeared in measures as the back door shut.

"That's it. I'm calling the cops," Chet said.

"Fine, but I'm going to see what those guys are up to." I glanced at Julia. "Are you coming with me or staying with chicken, here?"

It was childish of me to goad him into doing what I wanted him to do. Calling names was right up there with pulling pigtails and putting a tack in your teacher's chair, but I needed time to find the letters. And now we had competition.

"All right," Chet said. "I'll wait, but if I see any guns, I'm dialing 911, and I don't care what you call me."

Julia, Chet, and I made our way to one of the windows on the right side of the house by the library. Light pierced through the pane into the darkness. We could hear voices but couldn't make out the words.

I pushed up on my tiptoes and curled my fingers around the windowsill, trying to see what Percy's captors were up to. Being vertically challenged, I couldn't see a thing. "Chet, give me an alley-oop."

He rolled his eyes but stooped and folded his hands together to make a pocket for my foot. Lifting, he almost catapulted me into the nearby bushes.

I scowled at him, but he raised an eyebrow daring me to complain.

"What do you see?" Julia asked.

The skinny man flipped through the pages of a book and then tossed it aside. The larger one bent over, searching through the piles that were dumped from Cyrus's desk drawers.

Percy sat in one of the Queen Anne chairs near the fireplace. His eyes grew wide when he spotted me at the window. He jumped up and down in his chair and motioned with his head toward the guy searching the books. It looked like a bad attempt at charades.

Then I realized it was.

Percy sat still, waited for a moment, then flung himself against the back of the chair and let his head droop to one side with his eyes closed.

Julia stood pinned to the side of the house. "What's happening?"

"Percy. He's trying to tell me something." I glanced down at her.

"What is it?" Chet asked.

"I don't know. Let me down," I said.

Chet lowered me to the ground more gently than he'd lifted me and placed his hand in the crook of his back. "Have you gained weight?"

I shot him a look but didn't answer. "Percy was making some crazy gestures."

"Like what?" Chet asked.

I motioned for them to come closer. "He kept nodding to the thin guy." I tried to imitate him. "and then he sat still—" I stiffened my body and didn't move. "—before closing his eyes and letting his head sag." My head bobbed, and I closed my eyes.

"Dead. He's playing dead." Chet took his phone out again. "The thin man has a gun. That's what Percy is telling us."

"Are you sure?" I hated to sound so unsympathetic, but I needed a chance to search for the letters to make sure they were gone and not hidden somewhere new.

Once the police got involved, it'd be harder—not impossible, but harder.

Julia grabbed me by my shoulders and looked me in the eye. "There is a man tied up and gagged, being held against his will by two armed thugs." She shook me. "And I want you to hear this. He is related to me. We *are* calling the police." She nodded to Chet who had the police on speed dial.

She did have a point. Percy White was one of her relatives, not the most popular one, but still kin.

Chet dialed the number, but the screen on his phone went black. "This can't be happening. I forgot to charge it."

"No." Julia's eyes were saucers again. "I'll never be able to live with myself if something happens to him. I'm already a basket case about Uncle Cyrus. I mean how many ways can a family reunion go wrong?" Julia paced. "First a thirty-year-old murder, then Uncle Cyrus in a coma." She huffed. "And now Percy." She pointed to the window. "I'm never hosting another family reunion as long as I live."

"Calm down. I'll call." I glanced toward Chet.

But he didn't say anything. Instead, he slipped his phone into his pocket and slowly raised his hands in surrender.

Now was not the time for him to be funny, and I started to tell him so, but he nodded to something behind me. I turned around to find the slim dude holding a gun. "Ah, Julia."

Julia stopped, catching sight of the guy with the gun. "Oh." She raised her hands, too.

The slim man waved his revolver. "Let's move it."

CHAPTER TWENTY-FIVE

The slim guy put Julia in the leather chair across from Percy, me in the leather chair in front of the desk, and Chet in the desk chair. He used zip ties to bind our hands behind our backs while the larger one held a pistol on us.

Percy rolled his eyes. If he hadn't been gagged, he'd have given us an earful. I wasn't too happy about the ordeal either.

"Have you found anything?" I asked.

The large man lifted his eyes to mine. "I'd keep my mouth shut if I were you, girlie." He gave me one of those threatening looks that is supposed to intimidate.

But for some reason, it made me mad. Mad that they were in here rummaging through Cyrus's things. Mad that they were trashing the place even worse than it'd been, and mad on principle. Who did they think they were? After all, we had a right to be here.

Okay, well, one of us had a right to be here, and they weren't even using her to their advantage. An idea popped into my mind from the sermon Sunday.

A house divided cannot stand. *Perfect.*

I caught Julia's attention and winked at her.

The slim man picked up the next book on the shelf where he'd left off and fanned through its pages. Finding nothing, he dropped the book to the floor. The copy of *Tom Sawyer* where I'd found the letter from Carol landed next to another classic, *Call of the Wild*. *The letters*. Some of which Carol had written and some of them she hadn't. Cyrus's kindhearted Mildred, Carol, Percy, the letters, and the goons standing in front of me. Yes, the puzzle pieces started to connect in my mind, and a glimmer of understanding emerged.

"Well, I don't know what you're looking for, but maybe if you told us we could help," I huffed. "But go ahead and do it the hard way."

"What are you talking about?" asked the skinnier one, turning towards me.

"This is Cyrus's niece. If you had half a brain, you'd ask her for whatever it is you're looking for. She'd have a better chance of knowing than this half-wit." I nodded toward Percy who gave me a heated glare.

Julia jerked her head in my direction and opened her mouth to argue the point. I shook my head and winked repeatedly, borrowing Gabe's habit. She raised her eyebrows and this time nodded.

"She told me the other day that Cyrus keeps his most valuable possessions upstairs in his bedroom."

"Amy Kate, don't. If they find the map, they'll wipe out Uncle Cyrus," Julia said.

This snagged their attention.

If we could coerce one of them to go upstairs and search, we might have a shot at taking out the other one. With one upstairs, even with our hands tied, we might stand a chance. We had to try. Who knew what these guys would do with us once they found what they were searching for? So far, not a single patrol car had passed our way.

"What do you know about the map?" The large one asked.

"Only that he collects jars to put money in to bury." Julia cut her eyes toward me, and I noted her crossed fingers on both hands tied behind her back. "And that he keeps up with where they're buried by plotting it on a map of the land."

The goon with the gun plowed through the books littering the floor and jerked Julia up by her collar. "Show me."

Rats. I didn't anticipate that he'd take her with him. This wasn't good.

He dragged Julia to the doorway that led to the entry hall to the staircase. She limped due to her injured ankle, trying to keep up with him. The soles of their shoes hit the wooden steps as they ascended the stairs, letting us know when they had reached the top.

So much for that plan. I couldn't stop wondering what the goons would do once they realized we didn't know anything about a map. My stomach knotted. I glanced over at Chet. His eyes widened, and he tilted his head toward the window.

The slim goon had gone back to shaking the books, fanning through them, and dumping them onto the floor.

Not understanding, I shrugged.

Chet let out a groan, and we both glanced over to where the thin guy stood. His attention was on the search.

Then Chet gave two sharp nods in the direction of the far outside wall. Someone was peeking in the same window where I'd stood moments earlier. It was the oily teen, Danny. All I could see of him was his head.

I scowled at the adolescent and tried to persuade him to move away from the window before the goon saw him, and he found himself in the same predicament as us.

But he didn't budge. Instead, Danny stood frozen, his eyes focused on his dad tied up and gagged in the Queen Anne chair.

Percy's face softened when he spotted his son, but within seconds, panic appeared in the man's eyes.

Danny pointed toward the front door and then dropped

from sight.

My heart raced. The stupid kid was going to get himself and everyone else killed. Then in the back of my mind, I remembered Gabe Cooper saying those exact words to me. Sitting here with my hands zip-tied behind my back, I had no right to judge.

I hated it, but somewhere along the way, I'd started to like this kid. Double rats.

The three of us waited to see what Danny would do. Surely the knucklehead had a plan. Maybe, he brought a weapon, or perhaps, some sort of diversion. A couple of bottle rockets or possibly an air horn.

Bam, bam, bam.

My heart fell to my toes. He knocked. On the door. Hopelessness washed over me. We were doomed.

Chet's gaze met mine.

Bam, bam, bam.

The thin goon froze in mid-motion.

Bam, bam, bam.

"Stay quiet or you're done for," he snarled. He dropped a brown hardback to the floor and pulled his revolver out of his belt from beneath his shirt. He marched across the library, kicking a few books out of his way. With a quick glance over his shoulder, he disappeared into the front hallway.

Another knock sounded.

I stood and lowered my arms behind my calves then stepped through, so my hands were now in front of me. Grabbing the elephant statue sitting on the corner of Cyrus's desk, I moved to the wall by the library doorway. Peeking around the corner, I saw the goon crack open the front door.

Chet followed my lead and grabbed something to use as a weapon.

"What do you want, kid? I'm kind of busy." The skinny guy stood with his body in the way, so the kid couldn't see into the house.

"My phone died, and I need to let my mom know where I am," Danny said. "Do you have a land line or a cell I could use?"

Chet appeared beside me.

The guy studied Danny. "Don't I know you?"

Chet glanced at me and nodded. That was my cue.

We ran full speed at the guy, knowing the one upstairs would reappear when he heard all the racket.

Chet grabbed the guy and slapped his zip tied hands over the goon's mouth, trying to keep him from yelling. Danny rushed in and pushed his arm down, aiming the gun toward the ground.

I held the statue above my head with both hands, waited until Chet was out of the way, and swung with all my might until it connected with the back of the skinny goon's head. He dropped like an anvil to the floor and let out a muffled groan. The antiquated revolver clanked on the wooden planks, causing it to discharge. Boom.

Footsteps hit the floor above us in quick succession.

Chet scrambled over the skinny guy's limp body to grab the gun. He snatched it from the floor and aimed it at the top of the stairs. When the larger goon came into sight, Chet held him at gunpoint. "Amy Kate, call the police."

"No need. I already did." Danny showed us the cell phone in his hand and beamed. "I did that before I knocked. I'm not crazy."

Julia took the gun from the big guy's hand and stepped behind him. She poked him in the back to encourage him to move. "Go on downstairs and have a seat in the library while we wait for the police to arrive."

At the mention of the library, Danny jumped over the man out cold on the floor and ran to free his dad.

I stayed to guard the guy in the front hallway while the others took the big goon into the library.

Moments later, sirens cut through the night air.

Officers Jane O'Neal and Pete Howard were the first ones on the scene. This wasn't my first dealings with them. The scowl on Pete's face when he spotted me said it all. "We ought to have a special code for you." He helped the man on the floor to a standing position, then escorted him into the library where everyone else had gathered.

"What happened here?" Officer Jane looked toward Chet for an explanation.

"You should start with these two first. They were the ones who brought the guns to the party." Chet handed the firearm over to Officer Pete who pulled out a pair of gloves before taking it.

Officer Jane motioned for Julia to surrender her weapon as well. Julia nailed the big guy with a dirty look before handing it over.

"They found us looking in the window," I said. "And dragged us in here before we could call for help."

A smug smile emerged on the teen's face. "So, by calling the cops, I saved the day?" The amusement in his voice grated on my nerves, but he was right. He'd saved all our hides.

"Yes," I admitted. "You saved us, including your dad."

Julia interrupted, "They had Percy tied up like a Christmas present. Bound and gagged." She pointed to her cousin by marriage. "Ask him what this is all about."

CHAPTER TWENTY-SIX

Gabe Cooper stood in front of me, arms crossed and wearing a frown that would've given Scrooge a run for his money. He'd arrived before the other officers started the interviews.

I squirmed in the leather chair in front of Cyrus's desk. "We were here in the orchard searching for the missing letters. Gary Martin had mentioned seeing a shovel in the kitchen Saturday morning. Since Cyrus buried everything else, I figured he might've buried the letters, so I had to see for myself."

"Hm," he grunted, not breaking eye contact.

Julia tried to help. "She was right. We checked the holes that'd been dug up the day Uncle Cyrus was attacked, and she found a piece of an envelope in one of them."

His dark brown eyes simmered as he glanced her way. "I have a hard-enough time trying to keep Amy Kate out of trouble, but every time I turn around, it's the two of you I find in the middle of things."

Julia pressed her lips together and didn't say anything more.

His gaze landed back on me. "You know better than to enter a crime scene. Anything you found I want turned over to the officer. Now." He moved away, running his hand across the back of his neck, and planted himself beside the Queen Anne chair where Percy sat.

I pulled the torn corner of the envelope from my pocket along with the coin and the pocketknife.

Officer Pete held open a plastic evidence bag, and I dropped my findings into it.

Danny, who sat in the chair behind the desk, jumped to his feet. "Wait a minute." He reached into the pocket of his basketball shorts and pulled out a knife identical to the one I'd put into the bag. "Can I see that?"

Officer Pete handed him the bag. "Don't remove it. We already have too many fingerprints on it as it is." He shot me a cold glance.

That's where I'd seen it. The knife in the bag looked like the one Danny pulled from his pocket.

"What's David's knife doing here?" Danny directed his question to his dad.

Percy shifted in his chair.

Gabe took the knife and the evidence bag from Danny and compared the knives. "These are identical down to the initials on them. Can you explain this?"

"I gave each of my son's a pocketknife last Christmas. Their initials are the same D.J.W." Percy answered Gabe, but his eyes were parked on his son. "David must have lost his when we were here the other day."

Julia snapped, "It was you. You're the one who hurt Uncle Cyrus." She moved past me, headed for Percy.

I wasn't sure what she would do, so I grabbed her arm. "Let's hear him out, Julia."

Julia glanced down at me, then back at Percy. "Fine." She leaned her hip against the desk beside my chair and pushed her hands into her black jeans pockets. "But if he's the one who put Uncle Cyrus in the hospital, I can't promise what will happen."

One of the goons cleared his throat. "Watch what you

say, Mr. White. We still have business that hasn't been settled."

"I'd be more worried about the charges you two are facing for kidnapping and assault with a deadly weapon than about any business you have with Mr. White." Gabe turned to Officer Jane. "Get these two out of here. Book 'em, and I'll interview them when I get to the station."

"Sure thing, Detective."

He waited until the officers left with the two thugs, then continued. "Go ahead. What happened?"

Percy leaned forward, resting his forearms on his knees. "After Cyrus brought those letters to the reunion and showed them to Carol, I had to find them. They were all signed with her name, but she didn't write them. I did." Percy's head hung low. "I knew if I didn't destroy them, they would make you think I had something to do with Mildred's death. But I didn't." His head jerked up, meeting Gabe's gaze.

"Why did you write those letters to Mildred in the first place?" I asked.

"The gambling," Gabe answered. "I dug a little deeper after our discussion today and discovered he's had this problem for a while, even before he and Carol married. Word is he's in debt to the tune of thirty grand."

"Yeah, but I've always been able to keep it under the radar. That is, until Cyrus showed up with those letters. Carol started asking all sorts of questions, then when those two guys came to town looking to collect on my debt, I knew Carol would start putting things together." He leaned back in his chair. His shoulders sagged with the weight of his confession. "She discovered my problem after we married and threatened to leave me if I didn't stop. I didn't want my son growing up without his stepmother, so I quit. At least for a while, but then ..." He shrugged.

"But how are the letters connected to the gambling?" Julia asked.

"Mildred gave me money," Percy said. "Of course, she didn't know it was me, or that I used it to pay off my bookie. I'd write her as Carol, asking for a small amount every few weeks, using bad sales at the car lot or an unexpected crisis as an excuse. And she'd always send it with a little extra." He shook his head. "She was too kindhearted."

"And you took advantage of that." Julia balled her hands into fists and planted them on her hips. "You're despicable. A complete waste of air."

"Hey," Danny cried.

Julia peered over her shoulder at Danny. "Sorry, kid. I shouldn't have said that."

"So, let me get this straight, you wrote to Mildred as Carol asking for money?" Gabe asked.

Percy nodded.

"How long did this go on?" Gabe asked.

"For a few years. But then she wrote saying she couldn't send any more money. That Cyrus had found out and didn't like it. I made another plea, explaining to her that she's the reason we were staying afloat."

"Then what?" Gabe tucked the evidence bag containing the knife into his suitcoat pocket and handed the other knife back to Danny.

"I received a letter after she went missing, dated the day before she disappeared. It had the money in it."

Gabe nodded and stroked his chin. "Let me understand this, Mildred told you that she wouldn't send any more money, but then you say she changed her mind?"

"Yes, but I knew you wouldn't believe me. And if you found my letter pleading with her just days before her disappearance, you'd think I had killed her."

"You're right. I do think you killed her," Gabe said.

I glanced over at Danny who stood behind the desk, his eyes riveted on his father, a red hue staining his cheeks.

"My dad's not a killer." The words came out hard like

concrete.

Chet peered up from the notepad in his hand. "No, kid, you're right. Why would your dad kill the woman who'd been giving him money for years? It doesn't make sense. Why kill the goose that lays the golden egg, so to speak."

"Tell me what happened the day Cyrus was assaulted," Gabe asked.

"Yeah, tell us about that," Julia chimed in.

Percy shook his head. "It was all a terrible mistake. Those two men found me, even though I'd left Missouri to avoid them. I needed money quick, and I'd heard about Cyrus's pickle jars from Carol." He sighed. "Plus, after Cyrus showed those letters to her, I had to get them back. So, I thought I'd take care of both problems at once.

"We saw Cyrus burying the letters and waited. When he left, we went to retrieve them. But before we finished, Cyrus returned and found David and me digging in the orchard. He came after us, yelling and wielding those crutches like swords. I pushed him off me. One minute he was all over us and the next he'd fallen and hit his head on one of the tree roots."

"How did he end up in the library?" I leaned forward, drawn into the story.

"David and I moved him in here once we realized he was still breathing. I went to fill in the holes so no one would know we'd been here, and David was supposed to search for the map in the house, then call for an ambulance, leaving him to be found. But then you showed up, and he didn't have time to finish the job."

"What about the blood on the shovel?" Gabe studied Percy.

"It's mine. I cut my hand on a jar I busted, digging. You can see the scab." Percy held the palm of his hand out for Gabe to inspect.

Julia looked as well. "Maybe the blood is yours, but you're the one who put Uncle Cyrus in a coma."

"It was an accident. I swear. I admit I shouldn't have been on the property, but I didn't mean to hurt Cyrus, and I didn't take anything that didn't belong to me in the first place."

"The letters?" Chet asked.

"The letters. I found them buried out in the orchard right where Cyrus had been digging. But as you can see, I didn't have time to find the map or any money before Amy Kate showed up. All I took were the letters."

"The letters were no longer yours once you mailed them. So, you're looking at larceny and possibly a felony for burglary. You have no idea how much trouble you're in. Where are the letters now?" Gabe pressed.

CHAPTER TWENTY-SEVEN

"I can't believe Percy White was responsible for putting Cyrus in the hospital." Flora leaned her elbows on the counter near the cash register and shook her head. "I just can't believe it. But it goes to show, you never know what lurks in the heart of a man."

"So true," I chimed in as I scanned the bar code on the back of the book, entering it into our inventory file. We'd been working all morning to put everything into the database and onto the shelves.

Flora held a cup of coffee in her hands but hadn't taken a sip in the last thirty minutes. The news of what happened Tuesday night had consumed her thoughts for the last two days. It was all she could talk about.

"I can't get over the fact that he burned the letters," she said. "I'm sick about it. I just knew there was a clue in those letters that could've put us on the right track to catch Mildred's killer."

Destroyed. Turned into little piles of ash and wisps of smoke. Percy confessed to burning the letters he'd found buried in the orchard, and according to him, he never did find a map showing where the pickle jars were buried.

Of course, I didn't expect him to give up the map if he had found it. Not with the serious criminal elements that were chasing him. It was his ace in the hole. I figured if they sent one set of goons, they wouldn't hesitate to send another. And I didn't like the fact that they knew about Uncle Cyrus and his pickle jar banking. For this one reason, I was glad Uncle Cyrus was tucked away in the Pine Lake Hospital, with a floor full of professionals looking after him.

"Guess you'll have to find some other way to figure out who killed Mildred, now that we know what happened to Cyrus isn't connected to her murder." Flora lifted the cup of cold coffee to her lips and took a drink.

"Yes, I suppose I will." I scowled. Now I'd have to look at the evidence from a different angle. I'd been so focused on the letters I hadn't followed up on any of the other information I'd gathered, like Gary Martin's move or the rumors of his marital discord or the head injury from the forensic report. I hadn't even checked to see if Elizabeth received any updates from the Huntsville team who were examining the bones.

How could I have been so shortsighted? Aggravated, I plowed through the next two boxes of the latest releases from our distributor and settled on a plan to visit Elizabeth as soon as Carter arrived for his afternoon shift.

While I worked through the boxes, my mind replayed the lecture I'd received from my father once he'd found out about the kidnapping. He'd showed up in person at the bookshop to deliver it, and boy, oh boy, was it a humdinger. It'd been a long time since I'd seen his face turn that particular shade of scarlet, but it didn't come close to matching the earful I received from Gabe Tuesday night after all the arrests had been made and Percy had confessed to burning the letters.

"You can't keep putting yourself and others in danger. Stay out of this," he'd roared. Asking me to stay out of Mildred's murder was like asking me not to breathe or swallow or blink. Impossible. Guilt flooded over me. I didn't want to disappoint him, but I couldn't and wouldn't let Julia or Cyrus down.

Close to lunch, my phone in my back pocket chirped. I pulled it out, and to my surprise, found Julia's picture flashing on the screen. She'd taken the day off from Whispering Pines to go sit with her Uncle Cyrus.

Holding my breath, I answered the call. "Yeah. I understand." I glanced over at Flora who stood with her eyes glued to me, her face filled with worry, so I smiled at her. "That's wonderful news. I'll be sure to let them know."

"What is it?" Flora asked the instant my finger hit the end call button.

"Cyrus is awake." I beamed.

Flora squealed. "Praise the Lord." She threw her hands into the air.

"Which reminds me. Julia said to tell you and Carter thanks for all the prayers. She knows you've been having your congregation pray for him. It meant a lot to her."

"My pleasure. Nobody wanted to see that old coot make his way to the pearly gates, at least not yet. We need him here too much."

"I know. He's our local folklore." I chuckled, remembering all the talk around town about Cyrus Jacobs and his peculiar taste in glass jars. "What would the natives have to talk about if something happened to him?"

"Exactly." Flora picked up a stack of books and pivoted toward the row of shelves where the fantasy novels were housed. "I'll get started on these."

"Thanks."

The door whooshed open, and Carter strolled in carrying his lunch bag and a thermos of tea that Maureen had made for him.

I took his arrival as my cue to visit my sister Elizabeth. If Mildred's murder wasn't connected to the family, then I needed to start hunting in a different direction, and for me it seemed that direction led to the past.

Elizabeth's receptionist, Tilley Simmons, waved me through ahead of the two men waiting in the lobby. I found my sister in her office with her stocking feet propped on the corner of her desk with a file in her lap, deep in thought.

I knocked so as not to startle her.

She glanced up from the papers and smiled. "Hey, I was about to call you."

"Oh, good timing then."

"I take it you heard Cyrus is awake." Elizabeth moved the file from her lap and plopped it onto her desk, then swung her feet to the floor.

"Yes, Julia let me know. Isn't it wonderful? I mean he can be a real pain, but ..."

Elizabeth nodded. "I know what you mean. He's a pain, but he's our pain. Speaking of pains, I heard you've been busy getting kidnapped." Mischief twinkled in her eyes. "Dad was fit to be tied when he stopped by yesterday. His face turned beet red every time he mentioned you."

I took the seat across from her and placed my purse on the one beside it. "Dad overreacted. I was fine. Nothing happened." The need to cross my fingers behind my back swept through me.

"Of course, what's a little kidnapping at gunpoint? A mere trifle." She shrugged. "You must have a guardian angel or something. One day you're going to get into trouble and not be able to get out."

"Are you done?" I asked. "I've already heard how reckless I am from Dad and Gabe. Even Alexia piled it on, telling me Grant needs his aunt alive. She's become good at the guilt trips. I don't need it from you, too." I slumped deeper into the chair.

"So, there is no way I can talk you out of pursuing this?" She asked.

"Nope. You know I can't quit. Julia and Cyrus are both depending on me. And Cyrus deserves to know the truth." I swallowed the lump in my throat at the thought of how close we'd come to losing him.

"Okay." Elizabeth held her hands up in surrender. "I won't mention it again. So long as you know the reason we're concerned is because we love you."

I nodded, knowing that was true for my family. But for Gabe, I didn't know if it was because he cared for me or because when I "helped," I made his job harder.

"So, I'm guessing you came by for a reason." Elizabeth leaned her elbows on the glossy wood desk and propped her chin on her hands.

"I wanted to know if you'd received any further information from the forensic team in Huntsville."

"Yeah." She swiveled her chair in the opposite direction. A credenza sat along the wall behind her, holding files, papers, and a laptop. She rummaged through the stack to the right of the laptop and pulled out a green folder marked with a crest and some Latin words. "This came in Monday." She placed the folder in the center of her desk on top of the other file. "Here is something you might find interesting. Seems they swabbed the injury to the bone and found some metal particulates in it."

"Metal? Like a shovel?"

"No. These were brass. Also, the injury was a weird shape, like a crescent moon."

"So, she was hit with something made out of brass that leaves a half circle." I straightened in my chair and leaned forward. "That could be anything."

"Yes, the forensic team is working on it. But at least the crime scene has been narrowed to Cyrus's property and the house. She wasn't killed somewhere else and then buried there. The location of the body, the particulates found on it, and the timeline tells us that."

"So, what are the odds if the police happen to figure out what the murder weapon is, that it's still on the premises? This seems like such a long shot."

Elizabeth picked up the folder and handed it to me. "Look at the pictures of the fracture. She was hit from behind, crushing in her skull around the wound. The angle of the blow does give us some information about the killer."

"What?" I took the folder.

"That the murderer has to be between five foot three and five foot five inches in height. The blow is too level. If the weapon had been swung by someone taller, the report says the skull would have shattered differently."

I studied the pictures of the skull, letting it soak in that this had once been Cyrus's beloved Mildred. The one whose dresses hung in the bedroom closet and whose jewelry box sat open as if she'd just left. "Do you think if we could locate the murder weapon, the forensic team would be able to get any DNA from it?" I asked.

"Maybe. There are so many factors. Was it washed? Was it used often? More than likely there wouldn't be any fingerprints like with the suitcase, but the killer apparently didn't think to dispose of the weapon along with the body. Which leads me to believe it was a crime of passion. Something that just happened in the moment."

"So, you don't think Mildred's murder was planned?"

"No, I believe she was packed and ready for the women's retreat, and someone came to see her after Cyrus left. And that someone is our killer." Elizabeth drummed her fingers on the desk. "Someone who didn't want Cyrus to know that they were talking with Mildred. So, they waited until he'd gone."

I popped up out of my chair and paced, studying the photo in my hand, my brain fueled by my feet. "Who other than Percy White would need to talk to Mildred alone?"

"Well, who are the suspects on your list?"

I was ashamed to admit I'd let my prejudice drive my whole investigation. Percy White had been my sole focus. Now, with him accounted for, my list of suspects looked like a limp piece of lettuce, wilted without much crunch. "Well, I've talked with Carol White and Julia's Great-aunt Emma, as well as Kelly Parnell and Beth Jackson, the women with whom Mildred was supposed to catch a ride. They claimed she never called them, but who knows?"

"They could be lying."

"I've also talked with Trudy and Gary Martin, and I had the strangest encounter with Trudy's sister, Jess Roper. She's quite the character." I stopped behind one of the chairs and faced Elizabeth. "So, you think if we could find the murder weapon, the forensic team would be able to pull the killers DNA from it?"

"Yes, if it's still there and hasn't been compromised. But like I said, the chances of that are slim to nonexistent."

"Maybe we don't need the weapon. Maybe the idea of the DNA is enough," I muttered and glanced at the written report, listing the items in the suitcase.

"No, I'm pretty sure we need the weapon, if it exists, to get the DNA," Elizabeth said.

I smiled, letting the idea that floated around in my mind take root. "Could I get a copy of this report?"

Elizabeth squinted and leaned back in her leather chair. "You're up to something. I can see the smoke billowing out of your ears."

"Can I have the report or not?" I asked.

"Yeah, I'll go make you a copy." She circled her desk and took the written report from my hand. Once she'd disappeared down the hall, I laid the photo of the skull on her desk and grabbed my phone from my purse. With a click, I made a copy of the injury and the shape of the weapon.

I didn't like the feeling of being caught unprepared with my suspect list. And in case my little idea didn't work, I needed a plan B, which would be finding the weapon. Plan A, well, if it worked, meant I wouldn't need the weapon because I'd already have the murderer.

FAMILY TWIST

CHAPTER TWENTY-EIGHT

Gizmo licked my face, announcing the beginning of a new morning, finally Friday. I stuffed my feet into my slippers and shuffled down the hallway to the pot of coffee waiting for me. Julia had gone back to work now that Cyrus was out of the coma and didn't need someone with him around the clock. But she'd mentioned last night she intended to visit him at the hospital this afternoon.

The aroma of the coffee helped me to pry open the slits of my eyes. Gizmo stood by the front door. Apparently, he needed to make a trip outside.

"Hey, Danny." I stopped. The teenager wasn't there to take Gizmo out.

I peeked around the kitchen doorway into the living room, half expecting to see his lank, body sprawled across our white sofa. But it was empty. He'd returned to the RV the night his dad had been taken into custody. Danny knew his mom would need him. Against my better judgement, I missed the kid.

Gizmo let out a bark, and I hurried to throw on some shorts and a tee-shirt so the poor boy wouldn't explode before I took him to the grass in front of our apartment. I snatched the leash with the doggie bags tied around it off the coatrack and snapped it onto his collar. The heat swallowed my breath the instant I opened the door, and before I took two good steps toward the front, sweat poured from my skin and soaked my shirt. Good ole southern living.

When I stepped back inside the apartment, my phone buzzed on the kitchen counter beside my mug of coffee. I bolted for the kitchen, leaving Gizmo by the door still tethered to his leash. "Hello?" I pinched the phone between my shoulder and chin and stooped, motioning for Gizmo to come to me.

"Hey, sis. Did I catch you at a bad time?"

"No, just doing dog-mom stuff. What'cha need?"

Gizmo strolled over to where I squatted and allowed me to unhook his leash. I rubbed the tufts of hair behind his ears. "Good boy. Yes, you are."

"Are you sure I didn't call at a bad time?" Elizabeth asked.

"No." I stood and found my mug of coffee next to the microwave. "I have a minute before I need to get ready for work."

"Well, I thought you'd want to know Cyrus has decided not to press charges against Percy. He agreed it was an accident, and since Percy swears he didn't take anything but the letters, Cyrus doesn't want to stir up any bad blood in the family. At least, that's what he told me."

"Really? I find that hard to believe. The man who punched Gary Martin in the nose when he moved back after years of not seeing him isn't going to press charges? What about the breaking and entering? And the trespassing?" Surprise seeped into my voice.

"Nope, he's not pursuing any of the possible charges. He wants to put this all behind him."

"Huh?" I opened the door to the microwave and set the mug on the glass plate. This didn't sound like Cyrus. No, someone got to him and played on his sympathies. "He must've hit his head harder than we thought."

Elizabeth chuckled. "Possibly, but that's that. Percy will be released later today."

In a way, I was relieved. For the kid's sake.

"What about those two stooges, Larry and Moe? What happens to them?" I asked.

"They're not as fortunate. Seems there are some outstanding warrants for their arrests in a couple of states. They're wanted for kidnapping and assault with a deadly weapon. Gabe said something about busted kneecaps."

"Good. I don't want to think what might happen if those two were released. Uncle Cyrus wouldn't be safe. They still believe there are pickle jars with money in them buried in his orchard." I forced a chuckle to sell the idea of how preposterous this was. And I probably wouldn't have believed it if I hadn't seen it with my own eyes the morning I found Uncle Cyrus.

An old-time car horn sounded in my ear. I pulled the phone away and checked to see who was on the other line. "Look, Elizabeth, I have a call from Carter. I need to answer it. I'll call you later. And thanks for the information."

"No problem, bye."

I swiped the screen and accepted the other call. "Hey." I lifted the hot mug out of the microwave and moved to the kitchen table. "What's up?"

"We have a problem at the bookshop." Carters voice sounded tight.

"Okay?" I melted into the chair behind me. "What's wrong?" The last phone call about trouble at the store involved a fire.

"Someone threw a rock through the front glass door."

"Oh." I started breathing again. "Is that all?"

Carter chuckled. "I forgot about the fire. In comparison, this isn't all that serious."

"Is there any inventory missing?" I grabbed two sugar packets and added them to the brew.

"Doesn't appear to be. Just the broken glass all over and ..." He hesitated. "a note."

"What does it say?" I asked.

"You'd better come down here. Check everything out yourself. If it were me I'd call Gabe but I'll let you make that decision."

"It must be some note." I eyed my mug of coffee, picked it up, and poured the contents down the drain. "I'll be right there."

Squaring my shoulders, I pushed the door open and tiptoed my way through the mess. Glass shards sprinkled the carpet by the front door, and the open sign laid on the floor crumpled.

"Wow. They took out the whole upper half of the door. I'm glad we live in such an honest town, or everyone would've been reading for free last night."

"I'm glad the weather held," Flora said, practical as always.

Carter stood with a broom in his hand. "I'm surprised the entire door didn't give way." He moved forward and ran the broom around the edge of the threshold sweeping the loose pieces of glistening glass into a pile. "I waited until you arrived before I cleaned it up. Thought you'd want to see it like I found it. I did snap a picture of it though, for insurance purposes."

"Good thinking." I rubbed my chin calculating how much this little act of vandalism was going to cost me and if it was worth involving the insurance company. "Who do you think did this?"

"Not sure." Carter dragged the broom across the short carpet, pushing the larger pieces into his pile. "Didn't Gabe say he had a report about some vandalism out at the campgrounds?"

"Yes, but do you think they're related?' I watched Carter kneel and brush the shards onto a dustpan, then struggled to a standing position. "Let me do that."

I tossed my purse into one of the club chairs by the long front window and said a little prayer of thanks that they hadn't thrown their note through that glass. *The note.*

"Flora, did you save the note?"

"Of course, we saved it. It was tied to the rock we found past the self-help shelves. A little to the left, and we would've had a real mess on our hands. It would've taken out one of the display tables." She shook her head and trotted down the short hallway to the back workroom.

I took the broom from Carter who retrieved the garbage can from behind the front counter.

"I don't like this at all." He looked at me, and his expression softened. "We need to call Gabe. Your protection is the number one priority right now, and someone doesn't want you looking into Mildred's death." He dumped the dustpan and handed it to me.

Pressing it flat against the carpet, I brushed the last remaining chunks into it. "Let me look at the note before we do anything. It's probably nothing. More than likely the kids from the campground expanding their horizons." I smiled at my humor, but Carter wore his father-knows-best look, so I let it go.

Flora returned with the rock and the note while Carter went to the storage closet for the vacuum to finish up the job.

"Here's the culprits." She frowned, handing them to me.

The rock was nothing special. Whoever chucked it through my front glass door could've picked it up anywhere. Surprisingly, the note was no different. It'd been printed on copy paper. No clues to be harvested from the handwriting like the gender of the sender. No clues about location because the paper could've come from anywhere in town, or out of town for that matter. Plain white paper with plain black ink and the message written in Times New

Roman, the most used font on the planet.

I sighed.

"Not any help, is it?" Flora picked up my purse from the chair. "I'll put this on your desk in the back."

"Thanks," I mumbled without looking in her direction. Then I plopped into the club chair behind me and studied the few words that occupied the page.

Let the past stay in the past.

No, it wasn't the kids. Now, I understood why Carter took it so seriously. The message was ominous and full of meaning, and for some reason it sounded familiar. Like I'd heard it recently.

The vacuum kicked on, and the roar of the beast drowned out the sound of the cars passing on the street. Added to the noise was the click-clack of the glass hitting the metal of the brush bar as it whirled around sucking up the pieces.

For me, the note confirmed that the killer was not part of the Jacobs family. The majority of them didn't live in the area at the time of Mildred's disappearance. The only one local in 1986 besides Cyrus was Great-aunt Emma, and what would she have against Mildred?

I popped up from the chair and joined Flora in the back workroom. "Would you mind making some coffee? I didn't finish mine at home, and I'm going to need it."

"No problem."

The file Chet brought me last week lay tucked under a pile of invoices on my desk. I pulled it out and slid onto one of the stools. Laying the file open on the table, I examined the articles and the accompanying photographs, then placed the note beside it.

The vacuum clicked off, and Carter appeared with it in hand. Eyeing the note, he asked, "What do you think? Should we call Gabe?" He opened the door to the storage closet and set the machine inside.

"Um, I don't think so. Let's wait. I want to give these

articles a good once-over before I involve him. There has to be something I'm missing or someone I've overlooked." I spread the material out on the table.

"I'll help." Carter pulled out the other stool and took a seat.

I handed him the pile of pictures that had run with the articles. "See what you can find in these."

"What am I looking for exactly?'

"Anything that doesn't fit." Turning to Flora, I asked, "Could you call Mr. Shine and see what he can do about the front door? I'd appreciate it."

"Sure, no problem." Flora hurried to the front to make the call.

An hour later, she checked on us to give us an update on the door and to see if we'd made any progress.

"I've read and reread all these articles." Disappointment draped over me like a scratchy old wool coat.

"Don't give up. You'll find something," Flora said.

Carter leaned back in his stool. "These photos are so grainy I've had to look twice at a few of these people to make out who they are. I know some of them because they still live here, but many of them I don't recognize. Maybe, you should go through them, Flora." He held the photos out to her. "You've lived here longer."

"Okay, I'd be happy to, but I've already been through them once."

"Yeah, but it's worth giving them a second look. I'll go watch the front." Carter stood and moved toward the hallway.

Flora sat in his seat and laid the pictures out in a line. She studied the picture of Cyrus and Mildred—the one where he was wearing his coat. "I've been thinking about what I saw that day when I was passing Cyrus's house and thought I saw him out front in the stand of trees that used to be there before the road expanded. And the more I've thought about it, the more I'm convinced the person I saw wasn't Cyrus. I'm pretty sure it *was* a woman."

"That's what I was thinking after what you said. That it was a woman." I picked up the note and shook my head. "Let the past stay in the past. I've heard someone say that recently."

Flora tilted her head. "That's not a common thing to go around saying."

"No, it was someone I talked to in connection with the case. Someone—" My eyes widened, and my heart pounded in my chest, excitement surging through me. "Actually, it wasn't one but two people who said almost the same thing." I thumped the note with my finger. "Let the past stay in the past."

I stood and hustled around the table, looking at the pictures in their neat little row. Picking up the one of the First Church socials circa 1986 right before Mildred's disappearance, I picked out the person who'd said those words to me. She sat next to Mildred, but her eyes were on Cyrus. Then scanning the other photos, I found the picture of the other lady standing beside her husband, who had a mole on his cheek.

Now, the idea that'd been brewing yesterday churned with the force of an Alabama tornado. It was time to set a trap to catch a lovely rat, and I knew what bait would do the trick. All I needed was a little help from some friends.

CHAPTER TWENTY-NINE

When I pushed open the heavy door, I discovered Cyrus Jacobs propped up against a stack of pillows in his hospital bed, his gray hair aiming in every direction. The image of Albert Einstein danced into my brain, and I smothered a giggle.

Julia sat in the chair beside him and motioned me into the room. "I'm so glad you came. I'm trying to convince Uncle Cyrus to tell me where he keeps the map to his buried treasure." Her lips curled up, and her green eyes twinkled with mischief.

"She thinks she's being cute, but this is no laughing matter. If Percy and his associates—" He puckered his lips as if the words soured in his mouth. "—think there's a map, I'll never get any peace."

"You could put the map in a safety deposit box in the bank. Or better yet, you could put the money in the bank." I placed a Snickers candy bar on the rolling table in front of him.

His eyes landed on his favorite candy, then lifted to meet my gaze. "This for me?"

"You're the only patient here."

"'Not for long. They're letting him go home Sunday," Julia said.

"Oh, good. That's perfect," I said.

Julia shot me a look but didn't ask.

Cyrus picked up the candy bar and peeled back the wrapper. "Yes, and I am glad. If they bring me one more cup of Jell-O, I might shoot someone."

"But everyone likes Jell-O," I said.

"Sure, on special occasions with fruit floating around in it. But not plain Jell-O for every meal. No, thank you." He frowned and took another bite of the Snickers. "But this, man, oh man. It hits the spot." He smacked his lips together.

I sat at the foot of the bed, making sure not to bump Cyrus's cast, and watched him enjoy his treat, trying to work up the courage to ask for his help. "So, are you going to put that map in a safer place, or are you going to be stubborn about it?"

Cyrus shook his head. "Can't be stubborn about it, and I can't put it nowhere."

"Why not?" I snapped, frustrated that he was being so cryptic.

"There's no map." He pointed to his temple and tapped it. "It's all up here."

"You're telling me that you know where every single glass jar is buried? Over forty years worth?" Julia scooted forward in her chair. "No way."

Cyrus grinned. "I do. I know where every one of them is buried and how much is in each one."

"No, you don't. You're pulling our legs. You can't," I said.

"Believe what you like. But I do, and there is no map." Cyrus shrugged and popped the last bite of his candy bar into his mouth.

"Fine. I believe you, but for Julia's sake and the rest of your family's, you need to write it down. What if this had gone south? All that money would be lying out there useless. Or worse, others like those goons would swarm the place with shovels in hand, and there'd be nothing anyone could do to stop them."

"She's right, Uncle Cyrus. It's dangerous for you and us if you keep all that money buried on your property. It's time to dig it up and put it to good use. Or at least, put it in the bank like—" Julia stopped.

"Like normal people?" he finished.

"Yes, like normal people. So, we don't have to worry about someone hurting you over it."

Cyrus scrunched his face into a ball of wrinkles. "Fine." He spat out. "But only because I hate hospital food."

I glanced at Julia. "I have a little favor to ask the two of you. I need help with an idea I have. Actually, it's more like a trap."

Julia tilted her head. I'd piqued her interest. "I'm listening."

"I don't know how I could help you in my condition, but I'm willing," Uncle Cyrus said.

"I've narrowed the suspects of Mildred's murder down to two people. But I don't have any proof other than a coat being too long, a note thrown through the bookshop window last night, and the motive. I'm pretty sure the motive is the same no matter which woman committed the crime."

"Oh, so you think the killer is a woman?" Cyrus noted.

"Yes, I'm certain of it because of the injury to the head." I almost said skull, but when my gaze landed on him, the word changed. "The blow was delivered at a level angle or one slightly higher than Mildred's height."

"How do you know this?" Julia asked.

"I stopped by Elizabeth's office and coerced her into giving me a copy of the forensic report. And maybe when she wasn't looking, I might have taken a picture of the photo that was in the report."

"Impressive. I told you she was the one I could count

on to get the job done," Cyrus crowed.

"So, what do you need from us?" Julia asked.

"I need to give Cyrus a welcome home party. Sunday morning. A brunch."

"How does giving me a party catch a killer?" Confusion played on his face.

"Tomorrow, Julia and I will invite the family and a few others to the party, letting it slip that the police are looking for the murder weapon. That they're sure if they can locate the brass object that was used, there will still be DNA on it."

"Is this true?" Julia's eyes widened.

"According to Elizabeth, it is possible. DNA can last for a bazillion years, but it's a long shot that the DNA hasn't been damaged. If the object has been exposed to sunlight or heat or even washed, the DNA may be gone. Then there's the fact that it's been thirty years, and the likelihood of him still owning whatever the killer used is slim. And of course, the obvious problem is we don't know what we're looking for."

"So, what's the point?" Cyrus folded his arms over the covers.

"The point is—the killer won't know all this, and she'll want to make sure the item is gone. And if the two suspects know that Cyrus will be home Sunday and we invite them tomorrow, then that only gives the killer one window of opportunity to retrieve the murder weapon. Tomorrow night. And I'll be there waiting to see which one of them shows up."

"Tricky. I like it. I'll come with you."

"No, not after what happened last time. This one I'm doing alone. I'll keep in constant contact with my mobile phone. Besides, I have my trusty pepper spray in my purse. It's never failed me," I said.

Julia squinted, and her jaw tightened, but she didn't argue with me.

"Tomorrow, I need you to invite Trudy and Gary Martin to the welcome home brunch, since they're staying at the Whispering Pines as well as Carol. I'll see that Jess Roper and Beth Jackson receive an invitation, too. Be sure to mention the DNA and the police's search for the weapon."

"How can you be sure this will work?" Cyrus asked.

"I'm not, but if it doesn't, we're no worse off."

"How will you know when they'll show up? They could go at any time. I could tell Carol at eleven and she could head straight to the house."

"I thought of that. The road crew. The killer won't take the chance of being seen by them. She'll wait till it's dark, and the crew is gone for the day. But to be safe, let's wait to issue the invitations until three o'clock. Then we narrow the window even more."

"I don't know if I like this, gal. You hiding out in my house waiting for a killer. It's too dangerous. I'd feel better if you told that lieutenant of yours so he could tag along."

Telling Gabe Cooper that I was hot on the trail of Mildred's murderer ranked right up there with getting a root canal. Not my favorite thing to do, but at times, a necessary evil. "It would be better if I did this on my own, but if it'll make you feel better, I'll let Gabe know." But not a minute before it was absolutely necessary because I knew he'd try and talk me out of it. "Besides, Julia will know where I am, and if anything should happen, I'm only a phone call away."

CHAPTER THIRTY

Julia sat on the white sofa in our living room glued to the *Cold Case True Crime* show she loved. It was an indulgence she allowed herself on Saturday afternoons after she got off work from The Whispering Pines Bed and Breakfast. Lately, she'd been so busy with her family and work she'd missed this little treat. And since I refused to let her come with me, she'd resigned herself to the thrill of secondhand crime solving.

I stood in my room gathering the needed equipment for my stakeout. I'd grabbed my trusty flashlight and my fully charged phone, not wanting to experience the dead-phone syndrome like last time. And I almost forgot my tablet to whittle away the time I'd be spending in the closet under the stairs, keeping an eye on the front door.

Before I threw the phone into my black backpack, I contemplated calling Gabe. The warnings I'd received from both my dad and Gabe rang in my ears. Then Cyrus's trusting face popped into my mind, and guilt splashed all over my conscience.

Fine. I pushed the familiar number on my favorites list and listened as the call went straight to voice mail. "Hey Gabe. It's me. If you could call me back, I'd appreciate it. I have some information that you might find interesting." Telling him I was going to Cyrus's house to catch a killer in a phone message didn't seem like the thing to do. I ended the call and tossed the phone into the backpack.

Julia had delivered her invitations to the welcome home brunch for Cyrus right before she left work at four. It was now almost five, and I needed to hurry. I'd never forgive myself if I missed the culprit altogether.

I'd slipped the young guy on the road construction crew an extra forty to keep an eye out and give me a call if anyone should show before I arrived. So far, he hadn't called.

Stuffing the rest of the items into the backpack, I threw it onto my shoulder and entered the living room. "I'm about to head out."

Julia turned from the screen where a murder scene loomed large. She pushed the pause button as the camera zoomed in for a close-up on a skull.

"I made you a treat to take with you and a thermos of coffee, since we don't know when the killer will show." Julia stood and trotted into the kitchen. She always thought of others—that's what made her such a great friend.

I set the backpack on the couch and picked up my purse from the coffee table. Unzipping the bag, I pulled my keys and wallet from the purse, along with the key Julia had given me to Cyrus's house, and tossed them into the backpack. No need to carry anything extra.

Julia appeared with a lunch bag and a thermos. "You're sure you don't want me to go? I could make a second snack in a heartbeat."

I shook my head and added the goodies to the contents of the black bag. "I'd never get over it if you were hurt on my watch. Last time was too close." Gabe and his words of concern popped into my mind. "but I'll keep you posted, and I promise if anyone even jiggles the doorknob, I'll call."

"You'd better. I'm going to be a ball of nerves until this is over." She looked toward the scene on the TV. "I probably shouldn't binge-watch this show while I wait. It'll only add to my stress." She reached for the remote to turn it off.

Glancing at the screen, something about the close-up of the skull caught my eye. "Wait." I dug my phone from the bottom of the backpack and walked closer to the TV. Pulling up the photo I'd snapped from the forensic report of the skull, I held the photo on my phone next to the frozen image of the skull on the screen.

The head wounds were identical. A crescent-shaped indention to the bone.

Julia stood behind me with the remote, peering over my shoulder at the two images. "Wow, they look the same."

"What did the detectives on the show determine made this?" Excitement surged through me. We might have found the murder weapon.

"I don't know. Don't think they've revealed what it is yet."

I cringed and noted the time. "I have to go. I need you to fast-forward through this episode and call me the minute you know what the weapon is."

Julia's eyes lit up. "Yes, ma'am. I can do that."

Grabbing the backpack, I moved to the door. "The minute you know."

"Got it."

~

The young man with the road crew let me park my car with the equipment down the road from Cyrus's. He'd waited for me to show and then gave me a ride to the house. I didn't want whoever showed up knowing I was waiting inside, and I didn't want the patrol cruiser that came by every couple of hours to know I was inside either. I definitely received my forty dollars' worth out of that deal.

Ten minutes later, I sat on the floor in the closet under the stairs with my gear spread out. Julia hadn't called yet. How long could it take for the TV detectives to figure this out? The urge to pace grew strong, but I needed to remain hidden. So instead, I put in one earbud and pulled up my favorite lite jazz on my phone, keeping the volume low. Closing my eyes, I leaned my head against the wall, ready to wait, listening for anything out of the ordinary.

My phone chirped in my ear, and I jerked to attention. I pulled the one earbud out and answered it.

"Hey, you're never going to believe what the murder weapon was." Julia's voice rose with excitement. "Not in a million years."

"Julia, I don't have time for this. The killer could be here any minute, and I'd like the chance to look at the weapon before she does."

"Right. Sorry," Julia said. "The weapon used to kill Mildred was a fireplace poker."

"That means the murder took place in the library. It's the only room with a fireplace."

"I know. And I'm certain that Uncle Cyrus's poker is brass. Who would've thought my binge-watching that *Cold Case True Crime* show would help to solve a cold case here in Pine Lake?"

"Julia, I need to go. I'll call you later."

"Oh, right."

Sticking my phone in my back pocket, I reached for my bag of supplies to retrieve my can of pepper spray. The instant I unzipped it, I realized my mistake. The pepper spray sat safely back at the apartment in my purse on the coffee table. Shoot.

There was nothing to be done. So, I opened the closet door and peeked out. The sun hung low in the evening sky. Light gray shadows played on the floor, but there was enough light to see without turning on any lamps. Easing out of my hiding place, I crept down the hall to the library.

Earlier in the week, once the police finished processing the room for evidence, Julia and her father had ventured over and cleaned up the mess. Now, the room appeared to be back to its original state. All the books stood lined up on the shelves, and the contents of the desk had been replaced. But a strange calm tainted the mood of the library.

So much had happened here. Cyrus laid out on the desk, looking more dead than alive. Percy kidnapped and held at gunpoint. Julia, Chet, and I and our own encounter with the criminal element. But now this room was the scene of Mildred Jacobs' murder—A murder that happened over thirty years ago and needed to be put to rest once and for all.

I marched across the floor to the fireplace. There it was. The brass poker that had ended the life of Cyrus's one true love.

How many times had it been used since that heinous deed? An everyday tool turned into a weapon of murder. I reached for it, afraid that somehow it would take a hold of me and cause me to do some awful act. Lifting the heavy instrument from the stand where it rested, I inspected it. Soot and ashes were smeared on the hook, the crescent-shaped portion of the poker that left the indention on poor Mildred's head.

The vibration of the phone in my pocket sent my heart into my throat, but when I pulled it out and saw Gabe's name on the screen, it slammed into overdrive. Why was he calling now? Had he found out what I was up to? Then I remembered the voice message I'd left.

Sound casual, he's just returning your call, I repeated in my mind. "Hey, what's up?"

"Not much." His tone sounded even and friendly. Thank goodness. "I noticed I missed your call. What did you need?"

"I take it you didn't listen to the message," I said.

"No, but I hoped you were calling about our date. I was thinking since Cyrus is out of the coma and Danny is back with his mom and dad, and the world seems to be holding together for the moment, we might go out on a date tonight."

"Tonight?" I yelped.

"It's short notice, but short notice might work better for us. As you've pointed out, planning something tends to get messy. One of us always has something going on."

If he only knew. I would've laughed at the irony of the situations if it hadn't been so dire. "I don't think I can." I glanced at the poker in my hand.

"Oh, do you already have plans? I thought you were keeping the weekend open to help Julia."

"I was but something came up. Actually, I'm—" The sound of footsteps on the front porch caught my attention. I slid the fireplace poker back into place, trying not to make a sound.

"Amy Kate?"

The squeak of the screen door being pulled open echoed down the front hallway.

In desperation, I looked around for somewhere to hide.

"Amy Kate?" Gabe's voice called sharp and crisp. "What's going on? Are you all right?"

"Gabe, someone's here," I whispered and crawled under the desk.

The front door slammed, and the steady click clack of high heels on the wooden floor announced the presence of the killer.

"Where are you? Are you home?"

The footsteps stopped.

Adrenaline rushed through my body.

Slipping my phone into my pocket, I chanced a peek over the desk.

There in the fading light of the day stood Trudy Martin, holding the brass poker, wiping it clean with a little lace handkerchief.

    I needed to act fast. I couldn't sit there and let her destroy the evidence, and if she left, it would be my word against hers that she'd even been here. Then I remembered I had an ace in my pocket.

    Standing, I spoke loud enough for Gabe to hear me through the cotton of my jeans. "Trudy, I thought it was you."

    She turned still holding the poker, her purse dangling from her arm. "What are you doing here?"

    "You must have heard the police were looking for the murder weapon and were close to identifying it and getting their hands on the DNA." I moved around to the front of the desk, so Gabe wouldn't miss a word. If I was going to die, I wanted to make sure Trudy Martin paid for it. "I figured you'd show up here at Cyrus's house." My voice came out twice as loud as normal. I half expected Trudy to cover her ears.

    "I should've known you'd be involved somehow. Didn't you get my note? About leaving the past where it belongs."

    "Yeah, I got your note, but I have this funny habit. You see, I like to help my friends find the truth. And the truth here is that you never could measure up."

    Trudy glared at me and smiled. "Oh, I measured up. It's Mildred who didn't meet Gary's expectations."

    "I'm not so sure about that. From what I've heard, Gary couldn't let go of Mildred. He loved her, and you, well, you were a consolation prize." I moved beside the Queen Anne chair, putting it between me and her, in case she thought about swinging that poker in my direction. I needed to buy Gabe some time.

    "You think you know, but you don't. Mildred clung to him like a disease that he couldn't be rid of, no matter how hard he tried. She wouldn't let him go. He was leaving for Texas without me, all because of her. And in true form, she came to see him a few days before he left. Then she kissed him—long and hard while I watched from the window."

"She didn't love him, Trudy. She loved Cyrus. You had to know that."

"No, she was planning to run away with him. She'd told the women going to the retreat that she'd changed her mind. But when I came to plead with her to leave Gary alone—to give us a chance to save our marriage, I found her standing right here by this fireplace with her suitcase packed. Ready to run off with my husband." Turning her attention back to the fireplace poker, Trudy slid the handkerchief down the length of the pole.

How I hoped and prayed Gabe was hearing every word of this.

"So, you picked up that brass poker and killed her, without so much as a thought?"

"Oh, I had thoughts. I'd often thought about how life would be without her around. And for a minute, I thought Texas was the answer, but when he told me he needed me to stay behind, I had no doubt it was Mildred's doing." She smiled and smoothed the skirt of her red flowery dress. "So, once I saw the suitcase, I did what I needed to do. I gave my marriage what it needed. A clean start without Mildred Jacobs in the way."

"I can't believe you did that. You came here into her own home and took her life." The horror of her coldness filled me.

"A good wife does what she needs to do to help her husband. He couldn't free himself, so I did it for him." She laughed. "Jess always says I don't have any grit. Boy, would she be surprised if she knew. Like she says, you have to stand up for what's yours." Trudy took a step toward me and tossed her purse on the seat of the Queen Anne chair. "Time for me to do what I need to." Taking the poker in both hands, Trudy swung it with the speed of a professional cleanup batter. Whack. The blow landed on the chair. Great speed, poor aim.

I sprinted to the leather chair, shoving it between us. "Trudy, you don't have to do this. You could give yourself up. Let the authorities help you."

Trudy scowled. "What makes you think I need help? I'm perfectly capable of putting my own house in order. Thank you." She lifted the metal bar, and swish, it passed by my ear, missing my head. Ducking, I moved to the other side of the chair and pushed it toward her. Up went the poker, and down came another blow. This time it landed on my shoulder sending searing pain through my arm.

"You remind me of Mildred. She squirmed a great deal after I broke her leg."

Holding my arm against my body, I rushed to the desk as she slung the metal poker onto her shoulder. The metal against her red floral dress looked eerily out of place. Desperate, I pulled the phone from my pocket.

"Don't do that, Amy Kate. It'll only make things worse."

"Help, Gabe. Help." That's all I could say before she ripped the phone from my hand and threw it to the ground. In one motion, she crushed it with the spiked heel of her shoe.

"You won't be needing that anymore." The gleam in her eye sent shivers down my spine.

"Look. We can work something out, I'm sure." I backed away from her and inched my way to the door that led to the hallway. "We're both reasonable." I passed the Queen Anne chair. "What would it take to forget all about this?"

"Do I look stupid? You'd never be able to keep a secret of this magnitude. Just like Mildred, you're untrustworthy."

The door to the hallway stood within reach. I pivoted and ran. Pain from my shoulder shot through me with each pounding step. I gasped, fighting back the tears.

The sound of car tires on the gravel driveway spurred me on. I glanced back and stumbled. Trudy raised the poker over her head, and with a crazed wildness in her eyes, she swung.

~

The next thing I knew, Gabe stormed through the front door and pulled me out of the path of the weapon. The hook on the poker slammed through the wooden planks of the floor and stuck, inches from my head.

"Amy Kate, are you all right?" Gabe pulled me to him and held me tight, shielding me.

Two officers pushed through the door behind him and grabbed Trudy before she could wrestle the poker free. Officer Pete pushed her to the wall while Officer Jane jerked her handcuffs from her utility belt and slapped them on the raging woman. Trudy Martin ranted like a rabid animal as the officer Mirandized her.

"Ouch, my shoulder." The pressure of Gabe's embrace caused me to wince. "I think my arm's broken."

He helped me up, since I couldn't put any pressure on my right arm and let me lean on him all the way to his Corvette.

Leaning on his car, we watched the officers escort Trudy to the squad car and drive off.

Alone, he turned to me, relief shining in his eyes. "You had me worried. I wasn't sure I'd make it here in time. What I overheard on the phone sounded intense. She would've killed you." His brown eyes filled with concern.

"Don't I know it. I'm sorry." Looking down at my shoes, I shook my head, ashamed of what I'd put the poor man through. "I should've told you what I planned, not called right before I came."

He cupped my chin in his hand and pulled my gaze to meet his. "And if I'd been too late ..." He let his words drift off before placing the gentlest kiss on my lips—a kiss that held a promise of something more. "We need to get you to the emergency room, but on the way, I want you to tell me how all this happened."

"But all my gear is in the downstairs closet." He unlocked the door and held it open for me to climb inside.

"The one under the stairs." I didn't budge.

He groaned. "All right, I'll go get it. First though, get in the car where I know you'll be safe."

I smiled and climbed in, the laughter building up in me.

"What's so funny?" Gabe asked, a slow easy grin spreading across his face releasing his dimples.

"The fact that you'd think I'd be safe in the car." I giggled. "Don't you even know me?" I stuck out my left hand, the one that didn't ache. "Let me introduce myself. I'm Amy Kate Anderson, trouble magnet extraordinaire."

Gabe took my hand, bowed, and kissed it. "Pleased to meet you. I'm Gabriel Cooper, a helpless piece of steel."

EPILOGUE

My pink cast matched the paisley dress I picked to wear to Uncle Cyrus's welcome home brunch. I have to admit I hadn't thought my plan all the way through when I suggested the get-together. It never occurred to me that we'd actually have to give one. But with the trap laid the night before, there wasn't time to contact everyone to let them know it had all been a ruse.

Thank goodness for Julia Jacobs' gift for baking. She and Miles whipped up a batch of yummies to die for. I hated that we all had to miss church, but Julia said it was the least she could do since I had put myself on the line to help her family not once, but twice.

Besides, when the brunch was over, the few Jacobs that still lingered in Pine Lake from the reunion would be free to go home, and in her words, that would be cause for her own praise party, no church service required.

I entered the library carrying a tray of éclairs and moved through the crowd of friends and family huddled in groups of twos and threes. My dad stood talking with Elizabeth. When he spotted me balancing the tray in my left hand, he shook his head and grinned. He'd come to the hospital last night to check on me and kept me company while I went through the process of getting my cast.

Chet met me in the middle of the room and grabbed one of the chocolate delights from the plastic silver tray, then took the tray from me. "So, you caught the bad guy, or should I say bad gal."

"Yep, when I saw the forensic report, and Elizabeth mentioned that DNA could last forever in the right conditions, I figured it was worth a shot to use that information to try and catch the killer."

"I heard she almost caught you." Chet's blue eyes twinkled, and a hint of concern flashed in them. "But I'm glad it turned out the other way around."

The heat of a blush threatened to match my cheeks with my pink cast. "Me, too. And thanks for those articles. They helped to narrow down the suspect pool."

"About that." He glanced toward Cyrus sitting in the Queen Anne chair, looking like a king holding court. "I believe you owe me one interview with the man of the hour."

"Let me see what I can do. But from the way he's acting right now, it doesn't look like it'll be a problem."

"No, it doesn't. Let me know when he's ready. I'll make sure the managing editor holds the front page that day for the story."

Alexia approached, carrying baby Grant in her arms and a diaper bag over her shoulder. She took an éclair from the tray. "You should pass these around. The natives are getting restless."

Chet took a bite of the one in his hand and nodded to me before he walked toward Uncle Cyrus with the tray extended.

"Nice look." Alexia tapped the cast with the hand holding the éclair and smudged chocolate on the pink. "Oh, sorry." She twisted, aiming the diaper bag at me. "Grab the packet of wipes. It should be on the top."

They were not at the top of the oversized sack, so I

stuck my left hand down into the depths of the bag, trying to move things with my one hand while Alexia held the éclair and baby Grant. I pulled a rattle, a bib, and a set of colorful keys out of the bag and tucked them under my cast on my right arm so I could maneuver the other items better.

"Here, let me help." Gabe's voice rumbled next to my ear. I hadn't seen him since he'd left me in my dad's care at the emergency room to go interview Trudy Martin. "What are you looking for?"

The baby leaned over and grabbed the plastic keys from under my cast, which sent the other items tumbling to the ground. Gabe caught them before they hit the floor.

"The wipes." I stepped back out of the way, and without any struggle at all, Gabe pulled them from the bag. It reminded me of a magician pulling a rabbit from a hat, one, two, presto. He opened the packet, tugged one free, and handed it to me.

"Oh, There's Flora and Herman. She's been looking for a book for me that's out of print. Excuse me." Alexia whirled around, nearly hitting my cast with the diaper bag. Gabe pushed the wipes back into the monstrosity before Alexia dashed away.

"She might have a house in there, but that's just my theory." I scrubbed the chocolate stain, but it didn't come out.

"You might as well get used to having it covered in stains and signatures because I'm signing it."

"Oh, you are?" I teased. "You sound very sure of yourself."

"I am. It's the least you can do for me since I saved your life." He took the wipe from my hand and pulled a black marker from his front blue jean pocket. "I brought my own weapon." He took my left hand and led me to the leather chair across from Uncle Cyrus.

"There you are, gal. I was wondering where you went off to." His wrinkled cheeks bunched, and a broad smile spread across his lips. Cyrus pushed himself to a standing position with his crutches. "Can I have everyone's attention, please?" He hollered above the hum of the conversations.

Everyone quieted. "I want to say my thanks to all you folks for coming out to welcome me back home. I also want to thank Amy Kate and my great niece Julia for helping to catch the real killer." Uncle Cyrus chuckled. "For a minute there, I thought I might be going to jail."

Laughter skittered around the room.

Julia appeared at his side, beaming. "And for a minute there, we thought you might not make it."

"That's right," called Thomas, Julia's father. "But we're glad you did."

"Here, here," Several added.

"Well, I just wanted you folks to know how much this has meant to me. After Mildred disappeared, it was rough. It's nice to feel like I belong to the community again."

"Belong? Shoot, you're the town legend," Chet said. "Let's hear it for Uncle Cyrus, the legend of Pine Lake."

A round of applause and cheering broke out. Cyrus hung his head, the pleasure of the moment shining from his face.

Julia helped Cyrus to regain his seat, and Gabe knelt beside me, taking my pink cast and gently placing it on the arm of the chair. "Don't look."

I turned my head.

He scribbled something, then paused and added another line. "Okay, you can read it."

I pulled the cast toward me. He'd drawn a big heart around the chocolate stain and written *I'm looking forward to Saturday night ... with all my heart.*

And now, so was I. No cancelling, rearranging, or excuses. This time I'd climb over mountains to make it happen. When I peered up, my gaze met his, and in an instant, I knew I'd be spending many, many Saturday nights with this man.

He lifted my right hand and placed a kiss on the fingers that dangled from the gauze. "Amy Kate, will you do me the honor of having dinner with me Saturday night? If you're not busy catching a killer, or babysitting your friend's family, or helping your own siblings?"

"Yes, even if all that's going on, I'll still have dinner with you because this time it's circled with my heart."

Made in the USA
Las Vegas, NV
31 May 2024